TILL DEATH DO US PART . . .

Conner Egan sat in the evergreen tree, his arms wrapped around the enormous trunk, and watched the scene unfold before him. She'd almost caught him, the girl who'd appeared so suddenly in the woods.

Conner tried not to laugh out loud as he watched her scream and flounder in the snow. Who was she, he wondered? Where had she come from? One minute he'd been alone with his intended victim; the next, she'd been behind him. There'd been something about her . . .

And then he knew.

It was the longing. A longing so sharp and true Conner had felt it even through his own need. An anguish that had streamed out of her as she'd watched Conner and his victim in their passionate embrace. A longing for the thing Conner needed most in the world. The thing that would free him and pay him back for all his years of suffering.

A longing for love.

I've found you at last, Conner thought. *I'll find a way to get close to you. Soon, you'll declare your love for me. And neither of us will ever be the same again.*

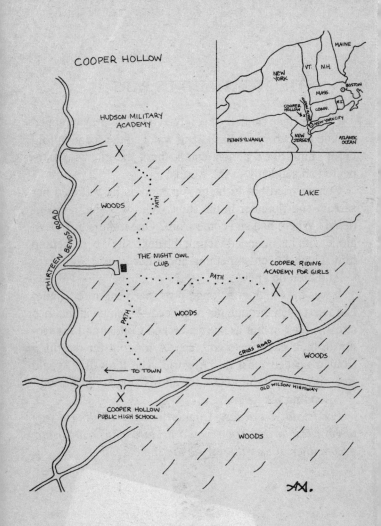

COOPER HOLLOW

HUDSON MILITARY
ACADEMY

WOODS

THIRTEEN BENDS ROAD

THE NIGHT OWL
CLUB

PATH

PATH

PATH

WOODS

TO TOWN

CROSS ROAD

COOPER RIDING
ACADEMY FOR GIRLS

WOODS

LAKE

OLD WILSON HIGHWAY

COOPER HOLLOW
PUBLIC HIGH SCHOOL

WOODS

MAINE

NEW
YORK

VT. N.H.

MASS.

BOSTON

COOPER
HOLLOW

CONN.

R.I.

NEW YORK CITY

PENNSYLVANIA

NEW
JERSEY

ATLANTIC
OCEAN

The Nightmare Club

#9: ETERNALLY YOURS

CAMERON DOKEY

Z·FAVE
KENSINGTON PUBLISHING CORP.

Z-FAVE BOOKS are published by

Kensington Publishing Corp.
475 Park Avenue South
New York, NY 10016

First Printing: February, 1994

Printed in the United States of America

Prologue

It was the night of the full moon.

The snow lay thickly on the tiny town of Cooper Hollow and on all the surrounding countryside. The trees in the woods looked like bloated monsters, their branches straining upward under the heavy mantle of snow. The lake outside of town was frozen solid. Its surface glittered, pale and deadly in the moonlight, everywhere but where it was covered by the hulking shadows of the trees.

Conner Egan thought it was the most beautiful thing he had ever seen.

He stood in the center of the lake, willing himself to ignore the tremors passing through his frame. Willing himself to believe they were caused entirely by the cold, and not by the excitement of what was to come. For this was the night of reckoning. The night he'd prove his love or die in the attempt. He had chosen to be here. It was too late to change course. If this was the only way he could have his beloved Julia, then so be it. And if he failed . . . he'd rather die than live without her anyway.

5

The thick silence of the woods was cut by the sound of horses laboring through the snow. Soon, Conner could see the white clouds of their breath as they neared the lakeside. Conner had brought no seconds to this pre-dawn meeting at the lake. But his rival, Richard Campbell, had one companion, wrapped from head to foot in a thick cloak the color of blood.

Conner watched as Richard brought his horse to the edge of the lake and carefully dismounted. Then, just as carefully, he stripped off his greatcoat and drew from his saddlebag a dueling pistol to match the one Conner held tightly in one hand. Without a glance at his companion, Richard strode forward onto the ice until he faced Conner in the center of the frozen lake.

Richard Campbell's features were harsh and strained in the moonlight. With his dark hair and stocky build, he looked like a cousin of the tree shadows spread across the lake. But Conner looked like moonlight itself. His pale hair was almost the same color as the ice beneath his feet. For a moment, neither man spoke.

"Richard Campbell," Conner said finally in a firm, strong voice. "For the last time, I ask you. Will you relinquish your right to claim Julia McKenzie as your wife? Will you step aside so that she and I may have a life of happiness together?" The other man made no response.

"You know Julia and I love each other," Conner continued. This time his voice was softer, more pleading. "Your marriage to her could be nothing but false. Why put us through this deadly charade? Relinquish your claim, Richard. Don't make me kill you."

Richard Campbell gave a short bark of ugly laughter. "You're awfully sure of yourself, Egan," he said. "I suppose you think because you're a hero of the war of independence and I'm just a Cooper Hollow farmer that I'll be easy to kill. But I think you'll find that you're mistaken."

"Richard!" For the first time, the figure on horseback spoke. Conner started as the figure slid to the ground and hurried toward them, the red cloak dazzling against the snow. It was Julia McKenzie.

"Richard," Julia said again. She reached out to grip his shoulders. Richard Campbell shuddered at her touch, but his face was as still as stone. "Why go on this way?" Julia asked in a low, compelling voice. "It's not as if you love me," she said, staring up at him. "If you cared for me at all, I would put a stop to this now. But you don't love me," Julia continued. "Do you, Richard? Can you tell me that you love me?"

Conner thought the world would stop while he waited for Richard Campbell's reply. Then, with one violent motion, the other man reached up and wrenched Julia's hands away from his shoulders, breaking the physical contact between them. Conner could see him gasp for breath.

"You promised yourself to me," Richard Campbell panted. His voice was choked with emotion. "I don't care what you feel for any other man. I intend to see that you honor your promise to be my wife. Now say farewell to your handsome young lover and get out of my way. I'd hate to shoot you both and reunite you in heaven."

Without a word, Julia McKenzie turned and fled across the ice. Conner caught her in his arms and held her close.

"I love you, Julia," Conner whispered against her hair. Julia gave a soft cry and clung to him. Gently yet firmly, Conner loosened her grip. He cradled her face in his hands. Julia's eyes were huge and brilliant, her cheeks flushed with emotion. Conner had never seen her look more beautiful.

"I love you, Julia," he said again. "I'll always love you." Conner raised his eyes to stare at Richard Campbell. "Shall I kill him for you?" he asked quietly. "I'll do anything to prove my love." Julia trembled and wrapped her arms around him once again.

"Conner," she breathed. "My brave and handsome Conner. I knew you were the one. I knew it." She lifted her face and drew Conner down for a long, slow kiss. "Don't be afraid, my love," she whispered against his mouth. "No one else can harm you as long as you love me."

"The choice has been made," Julia called out suddenly. She stepped out of the shelter of Conner's arms and walked to the side of the lake, her red cloak billowing out around her as she moved. Then she turned to the two rivals. Her face was lit in an astonishing smile.

"May the best man win," she said.

Without hesitation, Conner Egan raised his dueling pistol and shot Richard Campbell through the heart.

They left his body in the middle of the lake, covered with Julia's blood red cloak.

Julia sat behind Conner on his horse, his greatcoat spread over both of them. He could feel her warm breath on his neck as they rode. Julia's and Richard's horses plodded along behind them. Except for the horses' hooves and the occasional jangle of harness, they rode back to the Owl's Head Inn in total silence.

Conner had hated the Owl's Head Inn and Tavern on sight. The two story brick building was ugly and squat. The trees surrounding it were gnarled and distorted. A

his blood. "Once I loved as you do now. And I swore the same vow. I swore I would love forever. I swore I would do anything to prove my love.

"And this is how he repaid me," Julia cried. Her face was twisted by pain and rage. "In this very room he drained my life from me and made me what he was. A monster. A vampire—with only one choice. To find someone to promise what I had promised. For only the person who would swear to love me forever could set me free.

"I've waited years for you, Conner Egan," Julia McKenzie said. "And once the change is complete, I'll be free! Free to live out the rest of my life in any way I choose. Once you've taken my place, I can have anything I want, Conner. The reward for my pain and suffering will be a mortal life beyond your wildest dreams. You'll become what I am, and I'll have whatever I want for as long as I live."

She stopped speaking, and Conner felt the room close in to claim him. It was inevitable. He knew that now. In a few more moments, life as Conner Egan had known it would be over forever. His life as a vampire would begin.

"Remember, my brave Conner," Julia murmured as she leaned over him. He watched her swallow in anticipation of what was to come. "You must find a girl who will swear to love you forever. Who will do anything to win your love. Only then can you claim her and be free. As I am now free!"

With a cry of triumph, Julia fastened her teeth into Conner's throat. This time, he had no strength left to resist. He could feel her drawing the life blood out of him in huge, hungry swallows. It seemed to Conner that his entire world was filling up with blood. The room was the color of blood.

His body was covered with blood. And his ears were filled with the sound of blood—his blood—sliding, thick and heavy, down Julia McKenzie's throat.

I will find her, Conner Egan vowed with his last mortal thought. His fingers closed in a death grip around the locket he had given Julia McKenzie, tearing it from around her neck.

I will find a girl who will swear to love me forever. No matter how long it takes. And, as the sun rises over this very room, I will hold my feast at her throat.

One

January 1993

"You love me!" Ingrid Bergman cried, flinging her arms around Cary Grant. Her glowing face filled the entire movie screen. Her voice echoed off the walls of the theater. "You love me. You love me."

In the very last row of the Cinema 4 movie theater, Mercedes Amberson felt the tears slip silently down her cheeks.

Mercedes had been looking forward to the "Golden Age of Love at the Movies" film festival ever since Christmas. She loved romantic movies. Her New York therapist said it was because she lacked love in her *real* life. Mercedes didn't really care what her therapist thought. All she cared about was a romantic hero and a happy ending.

Her best friend at the Cooper Riding Academy for Girls, Andrea Burgess, had done a piece on the film festival for the school newspaper. Andrea's articles had been wonderful, full of interesting tidbits about the making of the movies and the lives of the stars. Andrea was great at digging out hidden information, finding just the right angle to

15

make her story special. Her writing talent was just one of the things Mercedes admired about her friend. Andrea also rode well, *and* she had a huge family that adored her.

Mercedes caught her breath on a sob and fumbled in her shoulder bag for a packet of Kleenex. Several of the little old ladies sitting further down in the theater turned around to stare. The big love scene was over. There was absolutely nothing to cry about. So why was she still sobbing?

Stop feeling sorry for yourself! she thought sternly as she wiped her streaming eyes. *And stop being such a crybaby. Anybody would think you were jealous.*

And she *wasn't* jealous, Mercedes thought. Not really. It was just that Andrea seemed to have all the things that Mercedes lacked. With a final sniffle, she wadded up the Kleenex and tossed it into her empty popcorn container.

Although both girls went to the prestigious Cooper Riding Academy for Girls, their backgrounds were entirely different. Mercedes was wealthy, like most of her classmates. But Andrea was one of the "new girls," girls who attended on scholarship, brought to the Riding Academy to enhance its academic reputation.

Scholarship girls were excellent riders, and Andrea was one of the best. Knowing the Riding Academy counted on her to help them win riding honors, Andrea frequently spent her free time putting her horse, Midnight, through his paces. With a big horse show just two weeks away, Andrea was spending her Saturday riding. She didn't have time to go to the movies. Something else for Mercedes to feel badly about.

Poor little rich girl! she thought. *I suppose it's just too bad you've got enough money to do whatever you want while Andy has to scrimp for every penny. And it's just too*

bad about your size six figure and all those designer clothes.

And it's just too bad, Mercy thought, as she watched Cary Grant kiss Ingrid Bergman, that money can't buy love. Once again, the tears began to slide down Mercy's cheeks. Because that was the one thing that Andrea Burgess had and Mercedes Amberson lacked. Andrea had people who loved her. And Mercy had nobody. Absolutely nobody.

Her parents certainly didn't count. She'd never made any real difference to them that she could see—except that she'd probably been considered an annoyance and a bother since the day she was born. Having a child had interfered with Dirk and Tanya Amberson's carefully pre-arranged existence: their annual trips to the continent and appearances at the dozens of social gatherings that made up their beautiful-people lives. Mercy's expensive therapist called her parents "emotionally unavailable." Her parents had been out of town at the time and unable to respond to the doctor's assessment.

The therapist had been worried about Mercy. Mercy needed to develop a more positive self-image, she said. To feel wanted and cared for. To feel loved. So she recommended Mercedes be allowed to spend more time with the one person who *was* emotionally available: her father's mother, Granny Amberson, who lived in the small town of Cooper Hollow, New York.

The credits began to roll and Mercy made a mad dash to beat the little old ladies to the bathroom. With any luck, she could stay hidden away until the second feature started. Then, her series pass would let her back into the theater. Coming up next was *Random Harvest,* starring Greer Garson and Ronald Colman. It was a film Mercedes had never

17

seen, but she'd read all about it. About how Ronald Colman plays a victim of amnesia who falls in love with Greer Garson. Then, in a freak accident, he recovers his memory and returns to his former life, never realizing that he's left his greatest love behind.

Safe inside the Cinema 4 bathroom, Mercedes ran water into the nearest sink and dunked a paper towel. She ran the soggy paper across her face, trying to erase all traces of tears. She should never have come back to Cooper Hollow after Granny Amberson's death. She knew that now. In fact, Mercedes had discovered her mistake the first moment she'd set foot in the Cooper Riding Academy for Girls. It wasn't that there was anything wrong with the *school*. It was Cooper Hollow. Everywhere Mercy looked, she was reminded of her grandmother.

Dirk Amberson had been all too happy to shake the dust of his small town upbringing from his feet. Once he'd left home for the big city, he'd never come back to Cooper Hollow. But his mother had stayed, loving the small town where she'd grown up. And she'd shared her love with her granddaughter. The times Mercedes had spent with Granny Amberson in Cooper Hollow had been the only happy ones she'd ever known. When the money from her grandmother's estate had made Mercedes wealthy in her own right, she'd found the courage to defy her parents' plans to send her to an upscale New York boarding school. Instead, she'd applied and been accepted at the Cooper Riding Academy. Even though Mercedes had never even seen a horse up close, she was determined to go to school in the one place she'd been happy.

But Cooper Hollow was empty without her grandmother. And Mercedes' natural shyness, her inability to make friends quickly, didn't help her at the Riding Acad-

emy. Even among the wealthy students of the Academy, she was considered rich. She had money of her own, not just her parents'. Most of the other girls quickly labeled her snooty and stuck up. Only Andrea Burgess took the time to find out what Mercedes was really like.

On the outside, the two girls seemed to have nothing in common. Mercedes was tall and willowy. Her long dark hair and dark eyes gave her a faintly exotic look. Andrea was a tiny blond. Her short-cropped hair and big blue eyes fooled a lot of people. It was easy to write her off as a baby-doll airhead. But Andrea Burgess had brains and guts. Shut out by most of her Riding Academy classmates because she wasn't from a wealthy family, Andrea kept right on going. She kept up her grades, wrote for the school newspaper, and she made friends with Mercedes, the other outcast of the junior class.

Mercedes gave her face a final swipe with the towel and tossed it into the garbage can. *Speaking of throwing in the towel,* she thought. If it hadn't been for Andy, she might have given up and gone crawling back to the cold comfort of her parents' house months ago.

The sound of voices outside the door alerted Mercy to the fact that the little old lady brigade had finally made it to the bathroom. Squaring her shoulders and plastering a smile on her face, Mercy held the door for the ladies as they trooped into the lounge. They chatted about the movie and patted their faces and hair.

"Oh, Mary Jean, we can't go yet. We have to stay for *Random Harvest,"* the lady in the lead was saying. She dabbed perfume on a handkerchief and applied it gently to her wrists. "I remember the day that film opened as if it were yesterday. It was the first time I'd ever seen Ronald Colman, and I thought he was the handsomest movie hero

19

I'd ever seen. And the story is *so* romantic." Mercy let the door swing shut behind her.

"Greer Garson follows him you know . . ." Mercy heard as she stood there for a moment. "Even though he's forgotten her, she sticks by him. Now that's what I call true love. You don't see that kind of devotion nowadays."

True love, Mercy thought, as she settled herself into her favorite back row seat with a second tub of popcorn. The opening credits began to roll across the screen, and the romantic music of the theme song filled the air. The little old ladies filed back into the theater.

"She sticks by him. Now that's what I call true love. You don't see that kind of devotion nowadays."

But I could do it, Mercy thought. Alone in the back of the theater, she gripped the container of popcorn so hard her hands began to ache.

If only someone would love me, she thought. *I'd do anything to prove my love.*

With a sudden explosion, the container of popcorn came apart in her hands, spilling its contents over the last row of the theater. The little old ladies began to fidget and whisper. But Mercy hardly noticed. She was entirely in the grip of the most powerful emotion she'd ever known.

I'd do anything for love, she told herself over and over again as she watched the pictures dance and flicker.

Anything for love. Absolutely anything.

20

Two

By the time Mercedes got out of the theater, the sky was growing dark. Alarmed, she checked her watch and saw that it was just a little after 5:00 P.M. With her stomach sinking in dismay, she realized her mistake. She would never get used to "country dark." It was so different from the dark of the city she'd always known. There were no street lights in the country. On quiet nights, not even the headlights of a passing car. Just moonlight and starlight with great huge wedges of darkness in between. And soon, there would be too much darkness between her and the Cooper Riding Academy.

It was too late to wish she'd done any of the other things available to her on a Saturday afternoon. Too late to think she could have gone to the indoor ring to practice with Andy. Or stayed in her room to do her school work. She even began to wish she'd joined the group of girls who'd gone shopping for the upcoming Valentine Ball.

The Valentine Ball was an annual event at the Riding Academy, following the February horse show. It was one of the few times the Academy opened its doors to students in the surrounding area. The event was a real "ball" in the

old fashioned sense of the word. Attire was strictly formal, and the Academy encouraged its girls to go all out. Many Academy students went in costume.

You didn't actually need a date to go to the ball, but Mercy wasn't about to stand around and be humiliated. She knew nobody would bother to dance with her. So why go shopping for a new dress? Now, though, even the company of her classmates seemed better than walking back to the Riding Academy alone.

But no, she told herself sarcastically, settling her shoulder bag firmly in place and yanking her hat down over her ears. *You had to go to the movies and wallow. Well, speaking of standing around, Ms. Amberson, it's high time you got moving!* Giving her shoulder bag a final tug, Mercedes left the comfort of the lights of Cooper Plaza and trudged toward the darkness of the road.

Though the weather had been clear that day, the snow was still piled in thick drifts all along the roads leading into Cooper Hollow. Mercedes' breath came out in big white puffs as she walked along. Within minutes, any sign of civilization was behind her, and she was deep in the Cooper Hollow woods. Walking on the road didn't really make Mercedes feel any better. In most places, the woods came right up to the road on one side and continued away from it on the other. The road was like an accident. A tiny fracture in the rows of trees. The only thing it did was to give her a firm surface underfoot.

Abruptly, something wet and sticky materialized from under the top layer of snow and attached itself to her boot. Bending down, she untangled a soggy paper flier from around her left ankle. She clutched it in her hand as she continued to walk along. The letters on the flier were easy to see, even in the dark.

22

NOW OPEN!
THE NIGHT OWL CLUB
Pool Tables, Video Games, Great Munchies,
Dance Floor, Juke Box, *Live* Bands On Weekend.

* * *

Bring A Date Or Come Alone . . .

* * *

Students From Cooper High School,
Hudson Military Academy,
Cooper Riding Academy for Girls,
Especially Welcome . . .

* * *

Located Just Outside Of Town.
Take Thirteen Bends Road,
Or Follow Path Through Woods.

* * *

Don't Let The Dark Scare You Away . . .

Yeah, right, Mercy thought as the flier began to disintegrate in her hands. Now there were soggy bits of paper stuck to her leather gloves. When she tried to brush them off, they stuck to her coat. *Don't let the dark scare you away . . .*

There was at least one fatal accident a year on Thirteen Bends Road. And all sorts of rumors of what went on in the woods. Or what *had* gone on. Frowning, she tried to figure out why the Night Owl Club sounded so familiar. And then she remembered. It was the place Andrea said they should go to hear live music on the weekend. The place with the weird history. Something about an orphanage burning down with all the orphans trapped inside. And Andy had hinted at spooky stories pre-dating that one.

23

Great place for a date, Mercy thought. Not that she'd ever have one. *Take the road of death or the woods of doom to the club of mystery. No two experiences ever alike.*

In spite of herself, Mercy began to shiver. She'd reached the place where she would have to leave the road to take the short cut. This was not a good time to be thinking about the spooky Night Owl Club. Still shivering, Mercy stopped walking and stood still for a minute to consider her choices. She wasn't very happy about either of them.

She could continue along the road until she reached the Riding Academy, a route that would take her another twenty minutes at best. And that would mean she'd have to walk up to the main entrance in full view of anyone who might look out a front window.

Mercedes squinted at her watch in the darkness. It was close to dinner time. That meant the Riding Academy students would be gathering in the dining hall for the evening meal. The entire student body would be walking by the big front windows that looked out over the Riding Academy lawns. The Academy had once been a grand hotel; Mercy could imagine the guests looking out and admiring the well-kept grounds.

She could just imagine how much her classmates would enjoy the sight of Mercedes Amberson slogging up the drive. "Stuck up Mercy" who didn't have any friends. Who went to a Riding Academy even though she didn't know the first thing about horses. "Poor little rich girl Mercy," whose money couldn't even buy her a date for the dance.

Better to leave the road now and cut through the woods. The way was shorter, colder, and scarier. But she could approach the school without being seen. Taking a deep breath, she started down the steep embankment.

24

The woods were even thicker than Mercedes remembered. The trunks of the trees seemed huge and menacing. And they were always in the way. She couldn't seem to find a pathway through them; she had to keep dodging back and forth, continuing in a straight line one moment, forced to veer to one side the next. The snow was deeper in the woods. The going was tougher. Within moments, she was wet and exhausted. More than anything, she wanted to be back at the Riding Academy in her warm, well-lighted room.

And then, to Mercedes' amazement, she wasn't alone. Just ahead she could hear laughter, a girl's laughter. And the answering chuckle of a young man. Even in the darkness, she could see quick flashes of color through the trees. Something red, she thought. A scarf? And the glint of pale blond hair.

Mercedes picked up her pace, hoping to catch up with the couple in the woods. It wasn't that she wanted to spy on anybody; she just wanted to feel safer, not so alone. Again, she could hear the girl's laughter. It was warm and coy. And then, silence. Veering around the trunk of a particularly large tree, Mercedes stopped short suddenly. The couple was standing just ahead of her, locked in a passionate embrace.

The girl was facing Mercy, her face hidden by the back of her lover's head. The guy had the most amazing hair Mercy had ever seen. An incredible, pale blond, almost the color of the snow. He wore it long, like a pirate in a swashbuckling movie. The red Mercy had seen was a silk ribbon holding his hair in place at the nape of his neck. While Mercy watched, the kiss ended, and the girl stared up at him adoringly. She reached up with long, tapering fingers to stroke his cheek.

Why isn't it me? Mercy thought suddenly. In spite of herself, she must have made a sound, for the girl had seen her. Her eyes grew wide, and she whispered something to her lover. Mercy jerked back into the shadow of the trees. She caught the quick flash of red as the blond head turned toward her. She couldn't tell if he'd seen her or not. In the next moment, she could hear the couple's laughter as they moved off through the woods. She was sure they were laughing at her.

Mercedes' cheeks were burning, and her chest felt tight. She hadn't meant to watch them. Hadn't *wanted* to watch. *But I can't help the way I feel,* she thought. *What's wrong with me? Why does everyone in the world have somebody to love but me?*

Slowly, she continued on toward the Cooper Riding Academy, all thoughts of staying with the couple for safety driven from her mind. Besides, she knew where she was now. Another few feet and she'd be out of the woods and onto the school grounds.

In the graveyard.

Three

The graveyard was hardly Mercedes' favorite place, even in the daytime. It was old, older even than the one in Cooper Hollow, if what Andrea said was true. The gravestones were pale and crumbling. They stuck out of the earth in strange directions as if the people buried beneath them were trying to force their way back out of the ground. Covered with snow, the stones looked like enormous bodies doubled over in pain.

Mercedes tried not to think about Sharon Cruise, the girl who had been killed here not long before Mercedes had come to the Riding Academy. Since Sharon's death, Riding Academy girls were forbidden to ride on horseback through the graveyard, and only seniors were allowed to walk there. But the graveyard continued to be used by those girls brave enough, or desperate enough, to take the short cut through the woods. The best way to get through it was to move quickly and not think a lot about where you were.

She was almost through the graveyard before she saw her. The girl from the woods.

She was sitting with her back to one of the stones, her

head down, her hands, with their long, beautiful fingers, resting quietly in her lap. Above her, a huge old evergreen tree swayed slightly. For a moment Mercy hurried on, her cheeks burning with embarrassment, anxious to avoid a repetition of the scene in the woods. It was probably just another lover's game. And Mercy had no intention of sticking around to see the conclusion. Though she didn't understand why anyone would want to just *sit* there in the snow . . .

And then, as Mercedes watched, a piece of snow fell from one of the branches of the tree overhead. She watched it fall, directly onto the girl beneath. It landed in her lap, completely covering her hands. And she never moved or made a sound. Even in the dark, Mercedes could see the pale white snow slowly turn a vibrant red.

Mercedes felt a horrible tingling sensation in the pit of her stomach. Her mouth and throat felt dry, as if she'd been walking through desert sand instead of winter snow. Her heart began to slam against her chest. Almost against her will, she moved toward the girl sitting beneath the tree. The only sounds were the ringing in her own ears and her feet sloshing through the snow.

This is a bad dream, she thought. *A nightmare happening to someone else.* Hardly able to believe what she was doing, Mercedes knelt down and scooped the snow away from the girl's hands. She scrambled for the girl's wrist, desperate to find a pulse. But she knew it was hopeless. No flicker of life met her searching fingers. The girl who had been alive just a few moments before was now very definitely dead.

Arms shot forward. Hands grasped the front of Mercedes' coat, and she screamed in terror, desperately trying to pull away. But the girl only tightened her grip, holding

on so tight Mercedes thought the bones would burst through the girl's fingers. There was a horrible sound of muscles scraping against bone, and as the girl lifted her head, Mercedes could see that one side of her throat had been completely torn away.

"Stay away from him!" the girl croaked. The girl's bloodshot eyes bored into hers. Blood flowed freely from her neck. She shook the front of Mercedes' coat until Mercedes' head rocked on her shoulders.

"If you value your life, stay away!"

Then, with one final convulsion, she pitched forward, burying Mercedes in the snow and covering them both with blood.

Four

Conner Egan sat in the evergreen tree, his arms wrapped around its enormous trunk, and watched the scene unfold beneath him. She'd almost caught him, the girl who'd appeared so suddenly in the woods. His need and hunger had given him away—almost. Almost, but not quite.

The moments of feeding were always the most dangerous. There was the hunger, so intense it drove every other thought from his mind. The pain and fear of the victim. The hot blood sliding down his throat. And then the moments of disorientation while he waited for the blood to take effect; to give him the power he needed to carry on. More than anything in the world, Conner hated and longed for this part of his existence. He put off feeding as long as possible, driving himself to the danger point before he chose a victim. Postponing the moment of feeding kept him lean and angry. Usually, it kept him alert. But today he'd let his hunger go just a little too far. Been a little too desperate for blood. A little too close to losing control.

It's this place, Conner thought, hugging the tree to him. He hated coming back to Cooper Hollow. But he always ended up here, determined to claim his final victory in the

place where he'd lost his hope, his love, his life. And always, when he came back, he pushed himself too close to the edge. Trying to deny the horror of the past and the truth of his present existence.

Conner scraped his face against the tree, trying not to laugh aloud as he watched the girl below him scream and flounder in the snow. Who was she, he wondered? Where had she come from? One moment he'd been alone in the woods with his intended victim; the next she'd been behind them, materializing from out of nowhere among the trees. And there had been something about her . . .

Conner searched his mind. Trying to remember the moment when he'd first become aware of her. Remembering now that, even through the haze of his hunger, there had been something about this girl that had attracted his attention.

And then he knew.

It was the longing.

A longing so sharp and true Conner had felt it even through his own need. An anguish that had streamed out of her as she'd watched Conner and his victim in their passionate embrace. A longing for the thing Conner needed most in the world. The thing that would free him and pay him back for all his years of suffering.

A longing for love.

This time he did laugh aloud, his voice a great cry of triumph from high up in the tree. But the girl below never heard him. Still screaming in terror, she scrambled from beneath the body of his victim and stumbled off through the snow. Desperate to reach the safety of light and warmth, the safety of other people.

Conner released his hold on the tree and plummeted to the ground. Fearless, now that he'd had his feast. Safe in

31

the knowledge that he was impervious to mortal injuries. He blew a kiss to the girl's retreating back.

I've found you at last, Conner Egan thought. *I'll find a way to get close to you. Soon, you'll declare your love for me. And neither of us will ever be the same again.*

Five

The hands still gripped her, strong and powerful. They shook her body back and forth. And now the horror called her by her name. *"Mercy,"* she could hear it say. Was it saying her name, or begging for something she could not provide? *"Mercy."*

"Mercy, for God's sake!" Andrea Burgess said. She stood next to her friend in the showers at the Cooper Riding Academy. Every nozzle in the shower room was turned on full blast. Andrea could hardly see Mercy for the water and steam. If she hadn't had her hands on Mercy's shoulders, she might have doubted her friend was really there.

Andrea hardly had been able to believe her eyes when she'd seen Mercedes come staggering up the Academy's back steps. Her face was pale and her eyes wild. Her clothing was sopping wet. Incredibly, she was covered with something that looked like bright red blood. Without a word, Mercedes had burst through a group of girls on their way to dinner, almost as if she hadn't seen them. For a moment, unable to believe their eyes, no one had moved. Then Andrea had scrambled after Mercedes while Helen Bledsoe went for Ms. Chalmers.

Something had happened. Something terrible.

Andrea found Mercedes in the showers, still sobbing and shivering in spite of the hot water streaming around her. A stream of bright red water ran from her clothes and down the drain. Andrea was just beginning to panic when Ms. Chalmers arrived.

"Mercedes Amberson, what is the meaning of this?"

Ms. Chalmers strode forward and turned off the shower nozzles. A group of girls crowded into the doorway.

"I asked you a question," Ms. Chalmers said. Water streamed down her angular face and dripped off the tip of her nose. Andrea had never seen her so angry.

Mercedes continued to sob and shiver. Her eyes focused beyond Andrea and Ms. Chalmers, on something neither of them could see.

"You have ten seconds to answer me," Ms. Chalmers said quietly. She counted backwards from ten, her voice low and calming. When she reached "one," and Mercedes still had not stopped crying, she raised her hand, palm open, and slapped Mercedes full across the face.

Mercedes' knees buckled and Andrea started forward, determined to catch and protect her friend. But the slap seemed to have done some good. Mercedes sat down hard on the floor of the shower room. Her eyes blinked rapidly and came into focus. She stopped sobbing, though she continued to shiver.

"Ms. Chalmers," Mercedes whispered.

"Very good," Ms. Chalmers said. "Now, if you're feeling strong enough, perhaps you can provide an explanation of this extraordinary behavior."

"Ms. Chalmers," Mercy said again. She stared as if she'd never seen the headmistress before. She looked around the shower room, seeing Andrea and the crowd of

34

girls in the doorway for the first time. She ran her hand down the front of her sopping wet coat.

"Oh, Ms. Chalmers," she said, her face crumpling with pain. "There's a body in the graveyard!"

Helen Bledsoe snickered. A ripple of nervous laughter ran through the girls clustered in the doorway. Ms. Chalmers silenced them with a look. Then she turned back to Mercedes.

"Of course there's a body in the graveyard, Mercy," she said slowly. "Lots of them. That's where they belong."

"No, I mean . . ." Mercy paused to catch her breath as the horror of what she'd experienced threatened to overwhelm her again. "I mean a *new* body. An unburied one."

"Mercedes Amberson, are you sure you know what you're saying?" Ms. Chalmers demanded, her voice stern but low. "I want to know the truth straight out. No fancy stories."

"I think she *is* telling the truth, Ms. Chalmers," Patty Harris said quietly from the doorway. Patty was head of the senior class and unafraid of the school's headmistress. "Her clothes looked funny when she came in. Red, like they were covered in blood."

Andrea spoke up for the first time. "I saw something red running down the drain, Ms. Chalmers. It could have come from her clothes."

The shower room was silent.

Mercy could see Ms. Chalmers weighing her choices.

"You two girls go upstairs and get cleaned up," she said finally, nodding at Andrea and Mercedes. "I'll expect to find the two of you in Andrea's room reading quietly by the time I get back.

"Mrs. Alcott," Ms. Chalmers called as she turned. The girls in the doorway scurried to get out of her way. "I

expect you to keep order while I'm gone. Ms. Saberhagen, you come with me. Apparently, I have no choice but to check on this myself."

Six

Mercedes sat upstairs in Andrea's room, wrapped in her favorite bathrobe and Granny Amberson's quilt. Andrea was curled up at the foot of the bed, glancing through a letter from her older brother, Bill. Her short blond hair stuck out every which way from her rubbing it dry with a towel. On her desk sat two mugs of hot chocolate, sending their fragrant steam into the air. For the first time in hours, Mercedes felt warm and safe.

"And then what?" she asked Andrea. Hearing about Andrea's family was one of the few real pleasures of Mercedes' life at school. To Andrea, a family of four didn't seem like anything special. But to Mercy, accustomed to boarding schools or private tutors, even one brother or sister would have been a joy. And Andrea's family was larger than life. They were always getting into scrapes; her older brother Bill was the most outrageous of the bunch. Getting out Andrea's family scrapbook and reading excerpts from Bill's latest letter had seemed like the perfect way to relax.

"Well," Andrea said, turning the pages of the letter over in her hands, "I think he blew up the chemistry lab."

Mercedes reached for her hot chocolate. "Does he say how?" she asked.

"Not exactly," Andy answered, stretching the suspense out as long as possible. Andrea made no secret of the fact that she thought Mercedes harbored a crush on her older brother. It probably helped that they'd never met.

"But he does mention something about chemicals that ignite on contact with water. I guess it wasn't really his fault."

"Andrea," Mercedes said, "this is your brother Bill we're talking about. You know, the one who 'accidentally' put his science project on reptiles and amphibians in your bed."

"Okay, okay," Andrea said with a laugh. "I guess I mean the school authorities have decided the explosion wasn't his fault." She took a sip of hot chocolate. "Well," she added, "anyone can make a mistake."

"Oh, sure!"

Andrea took another sip of chocolate. Mercy could feel her friend's blue eyes watching her over the rim of the cup.

"Merce," Andy said softly. "Are you all right?"

"I'm all right," she answered.

Andrea was silent for a moment. "Do you want to talk about it?" she asked.

"Oh, Andy!" Mercedes caught her breath on a sob. "It was so awful!"

The sound of a siren wailed through the night. A moment later, Mercedes and Andrea could see the flashing red lights of the paramedic van as it rolled up the Riding Academy's main drive on its way to the old graveyard. Right behind it, came a dark, four-door sedan.

Ms. Chalmers had objected to the police interviewing the girls in Andrea's bedroom. But Officer Montoya, one of the few women on the squad, had finally persuaded her that it was best for the police to talk to them where the girls felt comfortable. Mercedes had already been through a lot that evening. Surely it would be better to let her stay where she was—unless, of course, Ms. Chalmers would like to come with Mercedes to the police station?

Now Ms. Chalmers, Officer Montoya, and Homicide Detective Priestly, were crammed into Andrea's room. The third member of the team, Officer Sam Murphy, was down in the graveyard supervising the removal of the body.

By unspoken assent, Detective Priestly let Officer Montoya talk to Mercy. Jacinta Montoya was a small woman with flashing green eyes and glossy black hair. She asked Mercy to call her Jackie.

"You full name is Mercedes?" Officer Montoya asked. When Mercedes nodded, Jackie Montoya smiled. "Are you of Spanish descent, too?" she asked.

"Oh, I doubt it," Mercedes said, unable to keep the bitterness from her voice. "I think my father named me after his first expensive car."

Mercedes could hear Ms. Chalmers' quick intake of breath. Even the police officer didn't respond. Mercedes wished the floor would open up and swallow her. She wished she'd been the one to die in the graveyard. At least she wouldn't have to sit here answering questions. She was being horrible, and she knew it. But she couldn't seem to help herself. Hot tears of embarrassment began to slip down her cheeks. Without a word, Andrea moved to sit next to her.

Officer Montoya produced a large white handkerchief. Then she continued as if Mercedes hadn't spoken. As if people sat in front of her and cried their eyes out every day.

"It's awful, isn't it?" she asked. "It's shocking to discover a body, particularly somebody so young." Mercedes mopped her face with the handkerchief and nodded. Officer Montoya's calm, steady voice helped her regain control.

"Mercy," Officer Montoya said. "I know you'd probably like nothing better than to go to bed and forget this whole thing. To go to sleep and hope that, when you wake up in the morning, you'll discover all of this was a bad dream."

Mercedes looked into Jackie Montoya's compassionate face. Once again, she nodded. Jackie leaned forward to take hold of her hands.

"But it isn't a bad dream, Mercy," she said. "Right now the aid car is taking that girls' body to the morgue. She's dead. But *you're* still alive. And Detective Priestly and I need your help. Think, Mercy. Did you see who was with her in the woods? Did you see anything at all that might help us?"

Mercedes took a deep breath. She twisted the handkerchief over and over again between her fingers. *I can't remember,* she thought. *I don't want to remember.*

"Try closing your eyes, Mercy," Officer Montoya said. "I know it sounds hard, but close your eyes and try to picture the scene. Now tell me what you see."

Obediently, Mercedes closed her eyes. Behind her eyelids, the images began to flicker. The girl sitting motionless in the snow. The shape of her hands. And then red, red blood everywhere. And the horrible sound of her voice.

How can I tell them? Mercedes thought. *How can I say a dead girl spoke to me?*

"All I see is red," Mercedes cried. "There's red on the snow. And in his hair. The snow is the color of his hair."

With a gasp, Mercedes' eyes flew open, and she stared at Officer Montoya.

"Who do you mean, Mercy?" Jackie Montoya asked. "Who are you talking about?"

"There was a guy with her in the woods," Mercedes panted. She could hardly get the words out through the tightness in her chest. "I never saw his face, only the back of his head. But he had pale blond hair. I'm sorry, that's the only thing I remember."

"Blond hair," Homicide Detective Ed Priestly said. He watched as Jackie Montoya skillfully turned the patrol car out of the main drive of the Cooper Riding Academy and onto Cross Road, heading back to town. "Do you know how many guys there are in this area with blond hair?"

Jackie glanced over at him. "It isn't much to go on, Ed," she agreed. "And it might not be accurate. That girl was pretty upset."

Ed Priestly gave a groan of dismay. "You're probably right," he admitted glumly. "What was it she said?" He turned on the car's dome light and flipped through the notes he'd made of Jackie's interview with Mercedes.

"The snow is the color of his hair," he read out. He shut the interview notebook and turned the light off with a snap. "Great!" he said. "Just what we need. A murder committed by the abominable snowman."

In spite of herself, Jackie Montoya smiled. "Let's wait to see what comes back from the lab," she suggested.

"There may be all kinds of leads we don't know anything about yet."

"Yeah, right," Ed Priestly said. They drove along in silence. "Any word from Sam about possible cause of death?" he asked finally.

"Well, it'll have to be confirmed, but right now the coroner's saying loss of blood," Jackie Montoya answered.

"Loss of blood!" Detective Priestly exploded. "Mercy Amberson found her only minutes after seeing her unharmed. She didn't have time to die from loss of blood!"

"Oh, time wasn't a problem, Ed," Officer Montoya answered. "One side of that girl's throat was entirely torn away.

"Don't waste your time looking for an abominable snowman," Jackie Montoya said. "If I were you, I'd start looking for a vampire."

Seven

The next week passed slowly and quietly. Mercedes' nights were punctuated by nightmares and her days by visits from the police. They came back several times to check the details of her story, but she had nothing more to tell them.

The third time Detective Priestly had asked her exactly the same questions, Mercedes completely lost it. It wasn't her fault that she couldn't remember any more about the guy she'd seen in the woods, she'd screamed at him. Why didn't the police try to catch *him* and leave *her* alone?

Detective Priestly had departed, convinced that Jackie Montoya's assessment of the situation was accurate: Mercedes was too upset to be a reliable witness. And he wasn't about to start questioning every blond guy in Cooper Hollow. He knew a dead end when he saw one. As far as Detective Priestly was concerned, Mercedes had nothing useful to contribute to his investigation. Her involvement in the case was over.

Only to Andrea did Mercedes reveal the full story of that night in the woods. Andrea listened in shocked silence to Mercedes' tale of the dead girl speaking to her. Mer-

cedes had seemed so certain that what she was relating was true, Andrea thought it best not to question her. Instead, Andrea had comforted her friend; sat with Mercedes through that horrible first night until she fell into an uneasy slumber. Neither girl referred to the incident again.

Mercedes was appalled to discover that her finding the body of a murdered girl increased her popularity at school. Her classmates seemed more eager to know her now; she'd become a sort of celebrity. Mercedes tried to keep a low profile, staying in her room or reading in the Riding Academy library.

When Saturday rolled around, Andrea decided it was time for action.

"I have two weekend passes," she sang as she entered Mercedes' room early that morning. Mercedes groaned and pulled the covers over her head.

"Forget it, Andrea," she said. "I'm not going out there."

"That's it, Mercy," Andrea snapped. She reached down and yanked the covers back with one quick motion. "Time's up."

Mercedes sat up in bed and glared at her friend. There were huge circles under her eyes from lack of sleep. After a week, she still looked frightened and miserable. She also looked determined to stay right where she was. Andrea sat down on the bed next to her.

"Look, Mercy," she said. "I know you've been through a terrible ordeal. I know this week has been awful." Mercedes opened her mouth to make a rude remark concerning people who made brilliant statements of the obvious.

"But you can't spend the rest of your life in bed!" Andrea said quickly, cutting her off. "Stop acting like a victim, for God's sake," Andrea said forcefully. "Besides, I need your help."

Mercedes shut her mouth with a snap. "My help?"

"Sure," Andrea answered. She settled herself a little more firmly on the bed. "I want to go to the Cooper Hollow library this afternoon, and I need you to go with me."

"Andrea," Mercedes said. "You do not *need* me to go to the library."

"I do so," Andrea insisted. "If you ever came out of your room you'd know that our fearless leader, Ms. Chalmers, has recently issued a new order. No one is allowed off campus, or even out of the building, without a partner. No more roaming around the Cooper Hollow countryside by ourselves. Not with a maniac on the loose and a dead girl in our graveyard," she added. She watched Mercedes out of the corner of her eye, wondering if she'd gone too far.

"Come on, Merce," Andrea coaxed. "I have to go to the library to do some research for an article for the school paper. Nobody else is going to want to come with me. They're all going to one of the big malls to shop for the Valentine Ball."

Mercedes was quiet for a moment. "You could go with them," she said finally. Andrea was dismayed to see that her friend had started to cry.

"Mercy," Andrea said, "I don't *want* to go with them. We talked about the Ball before, remember? I can't afford a fancy dress I'll only wear once. And nobody's going to ask me to dance anyway. I want you to come to Cooper Hollow with me," Andrea said firmly. "You don't have to hang out in the archives and get all dusty. Sit in one of the alcoves and read a trashy romance or something. Just come to the library while I do my research."

When Mercedes still didn't respond, Andrea put her hand on her friend's arm. "We can make a special stop on

45

the way ho-ome," she said, trying to sound just like her mother offering a treat. In spite of herself, Mercedes smiled.

"You sound like an idiot," she said.

"That's because *you're* acting like one," Andrea answered.

The two friends looked at one another for a moment.

"Okay, okay," Mercedes finally said. "I give in. I promise to leave the safety of my room for the big bad town of Cooper Hollow. What time do you want to go?"

"Right after our delicious, nutritious school lunch," Andrea answered, bouncing off the bed. "We won't be home until late. And we're going to need lots of sustenance if we're stopping at the Nightmare Club."

"The Nightmare Club," Mercedes cried. "Wait a minute! What's that?"

"It's your treat for coming to the library with me," Andrea said from the doorway.

"Forget it, Andrea," Mercedes said, settling herself more firmly beneath the covers. "I'm not going anywhere near a place called the Nightmare Club."

"Mercy," Andrea replied, "don't you have a life? I'm talking about the Night *Owl* Club. That place I've been trying to get you to for months. There's a cool new band called Elysian Fields playing there. They opened last night and already everybody's raving about them. If we stop at the Club, I can cover them for the paper and kill two stories with one trip."

"But I've never *been* to the Night Owl Club," Mercedes said. She remembered now. The place with the spooky history. And the flyer she'd found on the way back from town. Right before she'd taken the short cut through the woods. *Don't let the dark scare you away . . .*

46

"Neither have I," Andrea admitted. "But you should hear the way everybody's talking about this band. Helen Bledsoe says the lead singer, Conner Egan, is the best looking guy she's ever seen. And you know she's already seen most of the guys on the planet."

Mercy choked back a laugh. "At least the ones whose fathers make over one hundred thousand dollars a year," she said. "I don't suppose this Conner Egan qualifies."

"No, but there's nothing like the thrill of a rock musician," Andrea answered.

This time Mercedes laughed outright. "How would you know?" she said.

"Oh, we ace reporters just know these things," Andrea replied trying to look smug and tough. She scooted through the doorway and into the hall as Mercedes fired a pillow at her.

"Meet me in the dining hall at twelve o'clock sharp," Andrea called over her shoulder. "And wear something you think will appeal to a rock singer."

Eight

The Night Owl Club was nothing like what Mercedes expected.

The outside of the club was the most uninviting place she had ever seen. A brick building that somehow managed to look ugly and squat in spite of its second story, set in the middle of a creepy grove of trees. The trees pressed up against the building like skeletons trying to keep warm. A pale blue light shone over the club's only door. It was easy to see how the Night Owl Club got its nickname. If Andrea hadn't been with her, Mercedes was sure she'd have chickened out and gone home.

But inside, things were better. Mercedes couldn't tell what was upstairs, but the downstairs had been converted into a comfortable combination dance club, game room, and snack bar. There were booths with low tables scattered throughout the rooms. Tiny candles in glass holders glowed, intimate and inviting. An enormous old jukebox stood in one corner, pounding out tunes until Elysian Fields came on to play. In the center of the ceiling above the spacious dance floor, Mercy could see a mirror ball already dropped down into place.

The club was packed. The combination of a hot new band and a Saturday night had drawn students from all over Cooper Hollow. A clump of guys from the Hudson Military Academy were clustered by the fooz ball table in the game room. Mercedes always felt a little sorry for the guys from the Military Academy, with super-short haircuts and ramrod-straight posture.

Most of the other guys looked pretty casual in jeans and tee-shirts and an occasional baggy vest. But the girls were dressier—lots of mini-skirts, crop-tops, and tight pants. Mercedes guessed it had something to do with the new band and Conner Egan. Hanging her coat up on a hook near the door, she looked down at her own clothing. Khaki pants and a plain white shirt weren't going to attract much attention. Not that the lead singer in a rock and roll band was likely to be interested in *her* anyway.

"Hey, Mercy," a voice behind her said. Surprised, Mercedes turned to discover Patty Harris standing nearby. Andrea had told Mercedes how Patty had spoken up for her to Ms. Chalmers. Spending a week hiding out in her room hadn't given Mercedes much chance to say thank you.

"Hi, Patty," Mercedes said. She wasn't sure what else to say. Did Patty really want to be friends, or did she want to cash in on Mercedes' sudden status as a celebrity?

Patty Harris scanned the crowded room.

"Andrea with you?" she asked. Mercedes nodded.

"Great," Patty said. "I told her she ought to check out Elysian Fields for the paper. Give us something interesting to read about for a change," she said as Andrea came up to join them. Patty gave Mercedes a friendly smile.

"I'm glad you came along," she said. "Some of us have a table near the band." She linked her arm through Mercedes'. "Come sit with us."

Before she knew what was happening, Mercedes had been drawn into the heart of the Night Owl Club.

It felt strange to be sitting at a table right next to the band. A table of privilege where everyone could see her. But Patty's open manner put Mercedes at ease. It was plain now that Patty had invited her over because she was genuinely interested in her, not because she wanted to attract attention to herself. Mercedes had always liked Patty Harris. She was warm and confident. For the moment, Mercedes, Patty, and Andrea had the table all to themselves. Patty's friends were off getting drinks or dancing.

"Forget about it," Patty said when Mercedes finally expressed her halting thanks.

"What happened to you was really lousy." Patty leaned across the table, her eyes sparkling.

"I hate to sound like a stage-struck female, but you simply are *not* going to believe this band," she said. "Every one of them could make *People* magazine's beautiful people of the year edition. But the lead singer is like nobody you've ever seen." Patty sat back in her seat and laughed. "It's the only time I ever agreed with Helen Bledsoe," she said.

The lights began to dim and the mirror ball slowly began to turn above their heads.

"Get ready," Patty Harris said. "Here they come."

"Are you going to sit there all night, or are we going to dance?" said a voice above their heads. Patty leaned back and smiled at the tall redhead looming over her. "Ready when you are," she said. She looked back at Andrea and Mercedes. "You guys know Mick Colombino, right?" she said.

"Right," Andy answered. Michael Colombino was president of the senior class at Cooper Hollow High. Of course he'd be with Patty Harris.

"Hi," Mercedes said as Patty slid out of the booth and onto the dance floor with Mick.

All around the Night Owl Club, the lights went out. Only the mirror ball continued to turn, sending brilliant daggers of light across the dance floor. The crowd held its breath. From somewhere, there came a steady drumbeat, like the pounding of a human heart. Then, with a crack that sounded like thunder, the drummer brought his sticks down across the drum's metal rim. The lights came up on the band platform, white hot and dazzling, just as the lead guitar began to wail. Elysian Fields had appeared from nowhere.

Andrea's jaw dropped. "I don't believe it," she said.

The five guys who made up Elysian Fields were dressed exactly alike. Skin tight black jeans and full white shirts that looked like clothes worn at the time of the Revolutionary War. The period effect was enhanced by their long hair, drawn back and held in place at the neck by black ribbons.

It could have been stupid and wimpy. It wasn't. It was lean and sexy as hell.

With one exception, all the guys were dark. Dark hair, dark eyes. But the guy standing in the center was unlike anyone Mercy had ever seen. His clear-cut features seemed to gleam under the hot white lights. His face was all angles—high cheek bones and a firm, strong chin. Even at a distance, Mercy could see his eyes, crystal green and blazing. His hair was pulled back from his face by a blood red ribbon. Hair the color of ice and snow.

Mercedes felt like she'd been punched in the stomach.

51

For a moment, she was afraid she'd be sick. In her mind's eye she could see it. The back of that pale blond head. The flash of red ribbon as the head turned toward her.

The guy from the woods.

"Mercy, what is it?" Andrea said. Beside her, Mercedes had begun to shake uncontrollably.

"I don't feel very well," Mercedes gasped. "I think I just need some air." But the room was so crowded, it was impossible to move. Staring out over the packed dance floor, Mercedes realized she'd never make it to the door.

"I'll get you something to drink," Andrea said. "Just stay here. Put your head down on the table if you don't feel well." She stood up and began to wade through the dancers, slowly making her way to the snack bar. In a few seconds, she was entirely lost to view.

It can't be him, Mercedes thought. *It can't be.* She put her head down on the table, blocking out the sight of the band. But in her gut, there wasn't any doubt. *The snow was the color of his hair.* How many guys could there be with hair like that?

All around her, she could hear the music of Elysian Fields pulse and wail. The room was incredibly hot. She was inside an inferno. The drum continued to beat out the same pounding rhythm as her heart.

And then, abruptly, it was over. With a final crash, the music ended and Mercedes was surrounded by the cheers of the crowd.

"Thank you, thank you," the lead singer purred into the microphone. "It's great to be back here tonight. I'm Conner Egan and you're listening to Elysian Fields." The crowd whooped and clapped.

"The guys would like to slow things down a little bit here," Conner Egan said. Again the crowd cheered, and Conner Egan smiled. "And I'll be back in just a minute," he promised.

Then, as the band launched into the slow, dreamy tune that was its second number, Conner Egan stepped off the band platform. And headed straight for Mercedes Amberson.

Nine

He'd known the minute she'd set foot in the club.

All week he had waited. Playing it safe, laying low. But the police seemed entirely baffled by the vicious crime in the old Riding Academy graveyard. As the week passed, he began to relax. No one suspected him. Now all he had to do was get close to the girl from the Cooper Hollow woods.

He'd lost a week. An entire week. But, with Mercedes safe inside the Riding Academy, there'd been no way to approach her. It couldn't be forced. It had to seem natural. He could have shouted for joy when he realized she'd entered the Night Owl Club. At last, she was near. And once he was with her, Conner was sure it was just a matter of time before things fell out exactly the way he wanted them.

But at the moment, something was terribly wrong. She had seen him, and she was scared to death. He could feel her fear radiating from her. Carefully weighing his options, Conner stepped slowly off the stage and headed for Mercedes' table. The closer he got, the stronger the sense of fear became.

He'd have to use the power, then. It was risky, but it was

worth the chance. Conner rarely used the special powers he'd inherited as a vampire. The ability to change his shape. And the ability to mesmerize his victims, to lull them into a false sense of security, to erase any sense of danger from their minds. He used that power only to feed. Only to assure himself of the blood he needed to carry on his quest for release.

The rest of the time, he preferred to use his natural abilities. His sharp wits and incredible good looks. Mercedes' declaration of eternal love, when she made it, must be what his had been. Straight from the heart and true. He couldn't use the power to influence that. It would count for nothing if he did.

Conner slowly made his way across the dance floor, acknowledging dancers as he went. He loved their attention. It made him feel sleek and powerful. He could feel their curiosity beat against him: Where was he going? Who was he interested in? He kept moving until he came to Mercedes' table. It was the first time he'd really gotten a good look at her. What he saw took his breath away.

She was beautiful. Long dark hair the color of wood smoke tumbled over her shoulders and ran down her back. The color was vivid against her plain white shirt. Her eyes were enormous. A rich warm brown, rimmed with thick lashes the same color as her hair. They looked up at Conner, wide and blank with terror. If he didn't act fast, he would lose her.

Conner Egan smiled. A warm engaging smile, designed to set Mercedes at ease. He could feel the power flowing through him. The wide, dark eyes continued to stare upward.

Easy, easy, he warned himself. He couldn't use too

much. Just enough to make her relax and forget her fear. And the reason for it.

"Good evening," Conner said. His voice was low and soothing. The power flowed over Mercedes like warm honey. She blinked and began to relax. Conner eased himself across the table from her.

"I'm Conner Egan," he said.

"I know," Mercedes blurted out. A slow blush spread across her cheeks. She still seemed tense, but now it was the tension of having said the wrong thing. The tension that comes from the fear of looking like a fool. Her hands were clasped tightly together on the table top.

She wanted him to stay. Conner knew that now. He smiled again, and watched her relax a little further. The blood began to sing in Conner's veins. It was going perfectly. The power was just right. In another moment, he'd have her where he wanted her.

"Well then you have the advantage of me," he said smoothly. He looked at Mercedes earnestly, holding her gaze with his vivid green eyes. "You know me," Conner said softly. "But I don't know you." He reached out and ran a fingertip along her hands.

"And I'd like to know you," Conner Egan said. "Very, very much."

Mercedes couldn't believe it. He was the best looking guy she'd ever seen. The guy every girl in Cooper Hollow was talking about. The guy they'd give anything to go out with. And he was sitting with her.

Mercedes stared across the table at Conner Egan. Her hands still tingled where he'd run his finger across them. Had he really just said he'd like to get to know her?

"Well," Conner said. He gave Mercy a charming, crooked smile and touched her hands with his finger once again. "Don't I even get to know your name?" he asked playfully.

"It's Mercy," she heard herself say. Her voice sounded funny. All breathy and light. "Mercy Amberson."

"Mercy," Conner repeated after her. And then he laughed. A rich full sound that showed his clean, white teeth. Mercedes' fears of a moment before seemed like an ugly dream. Why had she been so afraid of him? All she wanted now was to keep him with her.

"How wonderful," Conner said. "How perfect. Come on, my angel of Mercy." He stood and pulled her up into his arms. "Let's dance."

Slow dancing with Conner was like nothing Mercedes had experienced before. The white shirt felt cool and smooth beneath her fingers. His arms around her were strong and tight. She could feel his warm breath as he rested his face against her temple. Mercedes stirred slightly in Conner's arms. She felt him lower his head and brush his lips slowly back and forth across her throat.

A ripple of interest ran through the crowd as Conner pulled Mercedes onto the dance floor. All around her, she could feel the girls glancing at her sideways through their long eyelashes, trying not to let their boyfriends see their interest.

They envy me, Mercy thought suddenly. *They want to be me.* And why? Because Conner Egan had his arms around her. Out of every girl in the room, he had chosen her.

Please, Mercy thought. She tightened her arms around Conner's shoulders. *Let this be real. Don't let it be a dream. Let him really want me.*

The lush, slow music came to an end. Conner made a sound deep in his throat. He raised one arm and signalled to the band. Immediately, they launched into another slow tune.

"I have to go back soon, my angel of Mercy," he said. "Duty calls, you know." He paused for a moment, swaying gently in time to the music. Mercedes could feel his fingers moving through her long, dark hair. "This may be the only break I get all night," he said at last.

Mercedes' heart began to sink. She knew what was coming next. He was going to say goodbye and walk away. Just like everybody else. He didn't really want her after all.

"Will you wait for me, Mercy?" Conner said. "I could walk you home." Mercedes lifted her head from his chest and stared up at him. Instantly, Conner backed off.

"I'm sorry," he said quickly. "I shouldn't have asked that."

"Why?" she asked. "Why not, Conner?"

Conner Egan laughed and tweaked the tip of her nose. "Because you just met me," he said. "You don't know anything about me. And because . . ." He paused, gazing down at Mercedes. She could see his clear green eyes grow cloudy with an emotion she couldn't identify.

"What is it?" Mercedes asked. "Have I done something wrong?"

Conner Egan laughed silently. "Wrong?" he echoed. "Oh, no, Mercy. You're doing everything exactly right." He sighed and she felt his arms tighten around her. She put her head back down against his chest. *I'm doing it right,* she thought. *He's not going to walk away.*

"I'm just afraid of moving too fast, that's all," Conner said. His quiet voice was for her alone. "I know guys aren't

supposed to say things like this, but I knew you were special, Mercy. I knew it the moment I saw you.

"Out of all the girls in the room, I felt drawn to you." He paused to clear his throat. "And I wondered if maybe you could feel the same way about me."

Mercedes stirred in Conner's arms, but he kept her head cradled against his chest. "Don't say anything right now," he said. "I want you to have time to think it over. I don't want you to feel like I rushed you into things."

Mercedes raised her head. *This isn't a dream,* she thought. *He really wants me.* Her face was radiant. She opened her mouth to speak, but Conner laid a finger against her lips.

"Hush!" he said. The sound sent shivers down Mercedes' spine. "If you want to meet me, leave just before the end of the last set. Wait for me in the trees just outside the club."

"I'll be there," Mercedes whispered.

Conner Egan smiled.

Ten

It took Andrea the duration of both slow dances to get their drinks. It might be winter outside, but it was hot in the Night Owl Club. And everyone was thirsty.

"Whew," said the young woman behind the bar, wiping the back of her arm across her forehead. She was probably in her early twenties, and her ash-blond hair looked damp from the warmth of the room. "I could use something to drink myself." She smiled at Andrea and ran a wet rag across the top of the snack bar. "What can I get you?" she asked.

"Anything cold!" Andrea answered with a smile of her own. She should have been grumpy from waiting in line for so long, but she wasn't. There was something about this woman she liked. And she had to admire her for keeping the snack bar going all by herself in the middle of the Saturday night rush.

"How about a couple of Cokes?" Andrea said. "No, wait a minute," she called, as the woman behind the bar turned to get her drinks. "Better make that a Coke and a 7-Up. The friend who's with me isn't feeling very well."

"Really?" the young woman asked. She came back to the counter carrying two cans of soda and two large glasses

filled with ice. She handed the drinks to Andrea. "I hope she's okay. Do you need help?"

"I don't think so," Andrea answered. "I think it's just the heat." She looked back toward the dance floor. Out on the crowded floor, Andrea could see the other couples making room for the lead singer from Elysian Fields.

Wow, Andrea thought. *He sure didn't waste any time. I wonder who the lucky girl is?*

She could see Conner Egan leaning down to murmur something to his dance partner. The girl lifted her head, her radiant face looking up into his. One of the glasses of ice fell out of Andrea's hand and hit the counter with a crash.

The girl was Mercy.

"Hey, take it easy," the woman behind the snack bar said with a laugh. Andrea turned back, her face puzzled.

"What's the matter?" the woman said. Andrea shrugged and tried to look unconcerned. She couldn't figure out why the sight of Conner and Mercy together should disturb her. But the fact was, it did.

"I guess my friend's suddenly feeling a lot better," she answered. She nodded toward the dance floor. "That's her out there with the lead singer from Elysian Fields."

The young woman behind the bar was silent for a moment. Her unusual violet eyes regarded the couple on the dance floor thoughtfully.

"Two Cokes," the guy standing next to Andrea said. The woman behind the bar went to get his drinks. She served several more customers and then came back to Andrea.

"A good friend of yours?" she finally asked.

"My best friend," Andrea answered. She dug around absently in her shoulder bag. "Her name's Mercy Amberson. We go to the Cooper Riding Academy."

"Oh, no," Andrea said suddenly. She slapped her re-

porter's notebook down on the snack bar and continued digging through her bag. "I can't find my wallet."

"That's okay," the young woman said. "This round is 'on the house.'"

Andy looked at her in surprise. "Thanks," she said.

The woman nodded toward Andrea's notebook, still resting on the counter. "You brought your homework to the Night Owl Club?" she asked.

"Well, sort of," Andrea admitted. "My name's Andrea Burgess, and I'm a reporter for the Riding Academy newspaper. Officially, I'm here to do a story on the band."

"In that case, I'd better introduce myself," the woman with blond hair said. She extended her hand across the counter. "I'm Jenny Demos."

"You're one of the owners," Andrea said in surprise, shaking Jenny's hand. Somehow, she hadn't figured an owner of the Night Owl Club would be hustling drinks behind the snack bar.

"That's right," Jenny answered. "My dad's around here someplace." Her eyes looked out over the dance floor to find Conner and Mercy. "So, what made you want to cover Elysian Fields?"

"The reaction to them, I guess," Andrea answered. "The entire Riding Academy's talking about them." She followed Jenny's gaze, her expression sober. "Particularly the lead singer, Conner Egan."

"You don't like Conner dancing with your friend," Jenny Demos said. Andrea looked back at her in surprise. Meeting Jenny's serious gaze across the counter, it occurred to Andrea that Jenny wasn't just making idle conversation. She really wanted to know the truth.

"I guess I don't," Andrea said. "I can't really explain it," she continued, looking at Conner and Mercy. "There's

62

just something about him . . ." She broke off and turned back to Jenny with a rueful laugh. "I must be the only girl in the room who hasn't gone crazy over him."

"Oh, I don't know," Jenny Demos answered. She was silent for a moment, absently running her rag across the top of the snack bar.

"I think it's a good thing to look beyond outward appearance," Jenny said slowly.

"Do you mean 'looks can be deceiving?' " Andy asked.

"That's right," Jenny answered. She looked at Andrea with a clear, steady gaze. "Looks *can* be deceiving," Jenny Demos said.

"Jenny!" The harsh voice grated across Andrea's ears, making her jump on her stool. At the far end of the snack bar stood an old man, his shock of white hair standing out wildly around his head. His eyes were dark and fierce. He looked like a mad scientist in a late night horror movie.

"Yes, Dad," Jenny Demos said quietly.

"Don't forget your responsibilities," her father said harshly. His eyes rested briefly on Andrea. "We have other things to do."

Andrea could feel the air around her crackle with tension. *What's the matter with him?* she thought. Then Jenny Demos sighed and the tension diminished.

"I know, Dad," she said firmly. The old man glared a moment longer, then moved away.

"Wow," Andrea said without thinking. "That's your Dad?"

Jenny Demos smiled. "Oh, he's not so bad once you get to know him. His bark is worse than his bite."

"I'm sorry," Andrea said, embarrassed. "I didn't mean—"

"Don't worry about it," Jenny Demos said. "So," she

continued, changing the subject, "if you're doing a story on Elysian Fields, you'll probably want one of their press packets." She reached beneath the counter and handed Andrea a paper folder.

"It never hurts to be prepared," she said at the surprised look on her face. Andrea picked up the packet and her notebook and put them both in her shoulder bag.

"When you've done your story on Elysian Fields, how about doing one on the Night Owl Club?" Jenny Demos asked.

"That's a great idea," Andrea said. The band wound down the second of its slow numbers and the couples on the dance floor began to break up. Andrea could see Conner Egan walk Mercedes back to her table, then head up to the platform to join the rest of the band.

"The Club has a pretty interesting history," Jenny went on. "I even have some books you could look through for background information."

"I'd better get back to my friend," Andrea said. She jammed the cans of soda down into the glasses. "Thanks for the drinks," she said.

"You're welcome," Jenny answered.

Andrea took several steps away from the snack bar before something made her turn back to Jenny Demos. The young woman was looking across the room at Mercedes, a worried expression on her face.

"Don't worry about Mercy," Andrea blurted out. "I'll take care of her."

Jenny Demos' serious eyes looked across the bar at Andrea.

"I'm glad to hear it," she said.

Eleven

It was cold outside the Night Owl Club. In the shadow of the trees, Mercedes marched back and forth, stomping her feet to keep warm. It had seemed simple to agree to meet Conner outside while she was in the warmth and safety of the club. Now, standing in the snow beneath the twisted, ugly trees, Mercedes wished she could have waited for him inside.

Outside it was cold and uncomfortable. The trees made strange noises, their branches rubbing and crackling together even when there was no wind. But she told herself it would be all worth it. In another few minutes, she'd be with Conner.

Mercedes felt a twinge of remorse as she looked down the path that led from the Night Owl Club to the Cooper Riding Academy. Andrea had been furious with her for agreeing to meet Conner Egan after the band's last set. She'd used almost the same arguments Conner had used against himself to get Mercedes to change her mind. Mercedes hardly knew him. It might be dangerous . . .

But Mercedes was still riding high on the fact that Conner Egan was interested in her. It was a great feeling, a

feeling she wasn't about to give up. She'd do whatever was necessary to be with him. Furious and fearful, Andrea had stomped off down the path to the Riding Academy, leaving Mercedes alone to wait for Conner.

She didn't have to wait very long.

A steady crowd poured out of the Night Owl Club as the band finished its last set. Mercedes pulled back into the trees, not wanting to be noticed. The trees hissed and snapped as she pulled deeper into the shadow of their branches. Their gnarled limbs, like ugly hands, reached down to touch her.

The crowd thinned and Mercedes started forward. She didn't want Conner to miss her, hidden by the shadow of the trees. But the sound of voices held her back.

"Did you see Mercy Amberson?" Mercedes recognized Helen Bledsoe's voice. "I mean did you *see* the way she just *threw* herself at him?"

"I wouldn't have said it was Mercy who did the throwing, Helen," her companion answered. "It looked to me like it was the other way around."

"Oh, Patty, come on," Helen Bledsoe said, and Mercedes realized she was speaking to Patty Harris. "Who'd throw themselves at a girl like her?"

"Which one was Mercy?" a guy said.

"The one I introduced you to with the long, dark hair," Patty answered.

"Oh, yeah," Mick Colombino said. He was just about level with where Mercedes was standing, hidden in the trees.

"I thought she was very pretty," Mick said. "And that guy from Elysian Fields sure thought so."

"There, see, Helen?" Patty said with a laugh. The group moved past Mercedes and off down the path.

66

"You guys don't know anything," Helen Bledsoe said. "He was probably just bored. I mean, he didn't pay any attention to her for the rest of the evening. And she sat there, staring at him with those big, stupid eyes. I would have been embarrassed to death."

They turned a corner in the path and were lost from sight.

Mercedes stood in the shadow of the trees, fighting back tears. What if what Helen had said was true? What if Conner was just making a play for her to pass the time? Nobody else had ever been interested in her. He probably thought she looked like a sucker. And now she'd be humiliated. Her life would be worse than it had been before. All evening, Mercedes had been unable to believe her good luck. She'd been waiting for the other shoe to drop. She got the feeling it just did.

Mercedes started forward, determined to get back to the Riding Academy as fast possible. She wasn't going to stand around and wait to be humiliated. But she was held fast, her scarf caught in the twisted branches of an enormous tree.

Startled, Mercedes tried to pull away. The scarf around her neck seemed to tighten as she struggled to free it. She gasped for breath, and the trees began to rub their branches together. Her ears were filled with a horrible clacking sound, a sound that made her think of enormous skeletons rubbing their hands in glee. And she was their victim.

With a sob of desperation she took her scarf in both hands and pulled down hard. Abruptly, the scarf came free, and Mercedes staggered backward. Her back struck something solid. Arms seemed to come from nowhere to surround her. Gathering her breath for a scream, Mercedes

felt herself being spun around. A hand came down across her mouth.

It was Conner Egan.

She collapsed against him, too grateful for his presence to wonder how he'd found her. Around them, the trees were suddenly silent. The only sound Mercedes could hear was the beating of her own heart.

"Mercy, Mercy," Conner crooned softly. His arms around her were sure and strong. "There's nothing to be afraid of. I'm here now," he said, lifting her chin with his thumb and forefinger.

"Come on, angel of Mercy," he said. "Let's get out of here." With his arms still around her, he guided her out of the trees and onto the path leading back to the Riding Academy.

Mercedes felt as if she was walking in a dream. The moon had come out, rising steadily above the tops of the trees. The snow glistened and sparkled in the moonlight. How could she ever have thought the woods were spooky? Mercedes wondered. The whole scene looked like something out of a fairy tale.

Conner walked silently, but he kept one arm firmly around her. She rested her head against his shoulder. Beneath his coat, one of her arms was stretched across his back. Their feet scrunched against the sparkling snow. Everything would have been perfect, if it hadn't been for Helen Bledsoe.

They were almost back to the Riding Academy before Conner spoke.

"You're awfully quiet, Mercy," Conner said. "Are you sorry you stayed to meet me?"

"No," Mercy blurted out. How on earth was she going to ask him if he was planning to make a fool of her? "It's just that . . ."

"Damn it," he said. "You heard her, didn't you?"

Mercedes jumped. "Heard who?"

"That girl who came out just ahead of me. You heard those nasty things she said."

Mercedes was silent. Conner stopped walking and turned her around to face him.

"You heard her, didn't you?" he asked again. This time, his voice was incredibly gentle. Mercedes felt her eyes begin to fill with tears. Miserably, she nodded her head.

"Damn." Conner held Mercedes tight against him. "I hate people like that," Conner said. "They always want to screw things up for everybody else."

"Look, Mercy," he continued. They began to walk again, Mercedes tucked securely under Conner's arm. "Because of the band, I travel around a lot. I never stay in one place for very long. You get to be a pretty good judge of people. And I meant what I said back there in the Night Owl Club. The minute I saw you, I knew you were special. Not like that girl who only cares about herself. But someone special. Someone who might be able to care about me."

They stopped walking, and Conner lifted Mercedes' face to his.

"Nobody's cared about me in a very long time. I was beginning to think nobody ever would again. Until I saw you. I know things are happening fast. But I didn't make this feeling up, did I? You do care about me, don't you?"

This was it. Her chance for true love.

"Yes," Mercedes whispered. "Yes."

Conner gave her an incredibly beautiful smile.

"My angel of Mercy," he murmured. "I knew you were

the one. How am I going to get through the week without seeing you?" Conner's voice was filled with longing and regret.

Mercedes' heart felt like it was being squeezed in a vise. Leaving the Riding Academy during the week was strictly forbidden, particularly since she'd discovered the body in the graveyard. But she couldn't wait a week before seeing Conner again. Now that she'd found him, she wanted to spend every minute with him. A week. She might lose him in a week. He might find someone new!

I can't let that happen, Mercedes thought. *I can't.*

"It's not impossible," she heard herself say. "Not if you're creative."

Conner laughed and ran his fingertips lightly across her face. "Are you creative, Mercy?"

She looked up at him. He was incredibly handsome in the moonlight. The answer to her wildest dreams. It didn't matter that she'd be risking her ability to stay at school if she snuck out to meet him; that they could send her back to her parents if she got caught. The only thing that mattered was being with him.

"I can be," she breathed, hardly able to believe she was being so daring. She sounded like a different person tonight. She *was* a different person. Because now she cared for Conner Egan.

"When shall I meet you?" she asked.

Conner's face grew serious. "You're sure, Mercy?" he asked. "I don't want you to risk yourself for me. I'd never forgive myself if anything happened to you. There was a time when—" Conner broke off. He seemed to struggle for control. His arms dropped from around Mercedes, and he moved away. With an instinct born of watching a thou-

70

sand romantic movies, Mercedes knew he was thinking about someone else. Someone he had loved. And lost.

A white-hot stab of jealousy went through her. She couldn't bear for him to think about anybody else. Not when he was with her.

"Nothing will happen to me, Conner," she said. "Not if I'm careful." She went to him and turned him around to face her.

"Just tell me when you want me to be with you," she said.

"I want you to be with me always, Mercy," Conner Egan whispered. Then, slowly, he pulled her into his arms and kissed her.

Now Mercedes knew she was in a dream. Conner's lips were cool and sweet. But they made her feel warm all over. She'd never been kissed the way Conner was kissing her. It made her feel beautiful and alive. It made her dizzy with happiness.

The kiss ended. She rested her head against Conner's chest and slowly came back to earth.

"What was she like?" Mercedes asked at last.

"Who?" Conner asked.

"The girl you were just talking about," Mercedes answered.

Conner gave a self-conscious laugh. "How did you know I was talking about another girl?" he said.

Mercedes shrugged. "I just know," she said. There was a tiny silence. She had to know. "You loved her very much, didn't you?"

Conner Egan didn't answer for a very long time. "Yes, I loved her very much," he finally said. "And I lost her. She had another boyfriend she didn't know how to break

up with. So she had to sneak out to meet me. I shouldn't have let her do it. But I did.

"One night she got caught on her way to meet me and—" Conner took a ragged breath. "Let's just say we didn't see each other after that," he finished quietly.

"Now you know why I can't let you risk sneaking out to meet me, Mercy," Conner said. "I hate to think of five whole days without you. But I can't run the risk of history repeating itself." He took her face between his hands and gazed down at her.

"You're special to me," he said. "I can't risk losing you."

She smiled up at him, glad she'd pressed Conner about his old girlfriend. Compared to what had happened before, her situation seemed so simple.

"But Conner, I haven't *got* another boyfriend," she said with a laugh. "There's no one at all here who cares anything about me, except for Andrea." Mercedes felt a twinge at the thought of what Andy would say if she knew what Mercy was planning. But she didn't let that stop her.

"It'll be easy for me to get out of the Academy," Mercedes said. "Nobody will be expecting it. They'll all think I stayed in my room, like I did this week." Unbidden, a tiny shiver ran down Mercedes' spine as she remembered the reason she'd hidden herself away. Feeling her shiver, Conner held her close.

"You mean it, Mercy?" he whispered against her hair. She nodded, and Conner tightened his embrace. "Will you meet me tomorrow?" he asked her. "If I could see you again right away, I could be sure."

Mercedes felt a cold tendril of fear enter her heart. "Sure of what, Conner?" she asked.

"I just don't want it to be like before," Conner said. "I

can still remember the last time I saw her," he whispered. "She was dressed all in black. She knew I loved her in black, and she wore it just for me.

"Oh, God," he said in sudden anguish. "I wish I could stop thinking about her. I wish I could forget what happened."

"I can help you forget, Conner." Mercedes could hardly believe she'd spoken the words that were racing through her heart.

"Please, Conner," she said, when still he didn't answer her. "It'll be easy for me to get away. You'll see. I'll wait until everyone's in their rooms after lights out. Then I'll come to the Night Owl Club. I'll be safe there, won't I?" Mercedes asked.

Conner drew her back into his arms and showed his gratitude with another kiss.

"Of course you will, my angel of Mercy."

Twelve

Crouched behind a tree on the other side of the path, Andrea was so pissed off at the way Mercy was behaving with Conner Egan she wasn't sure whether she'd freeze to death or go up in angry flames.

How can she buy that stuff? Andrea thought, listening in disbelief as Conner spun his tale of lost love. Andrea knew that Mercedes longed for a boyfriend, but she would never have expected her friend to agree to sneak out of the Riding Academy to meet a guy she'd just met. It just wasn't like her. And why couldn't Mercy see that all Conner was doing was feeding her a line?

Andrea had been halfway back to the Riding Academy before she'd realized there was still a way she could make sure Mercedes was safe, even if she couldn't talk her out of walking home with Conner Egan. All she had to do was find a good hiding place somewhere along the path between the Riding Academy and the Night Owl Club and wait for the couple to come along. Once she'd seen her friend was all right, and once she'd seen Conner leave, Andrea could follow Mercy home and nobody would be the wiser. Andrea didn't really like the thought of spying

on her friend, but it was better than worrying about whether or not Mercy was safe.

A silence had fallen on the other side of the path, and Andrea was sure Conner and Mercy were wrapped in another embrace. She tried to imagine kissing Conner Egan. Just thinking about it made her sick.

What is *it about him I don't like?* Andrea wondered again. And again, she didn't have an answer. There was just something about him that wasn't quite right. Something hidden just below the surface. Andrea had a feeling that whatever was below the surface was the true Conner Egan. All the stuff on top was just for show.

Andrea's legs began to protest their crouched position in the snow. She wished Conner and Mercy would hurry up so they could all go home.

As if they'd heard her, the two finally parted. She could hear them say goodnight. Then Mercedes continued along the path to the Riding Academy, and Andrea could hear Conner moving off in the opposite direction. She waited until Conner's footsteps faded away, then stood up and watched her friend until she was out of sight. Only then did Andrea breath a little easier. Nothing terrible had happened to Mercy. Unless you counted Conner's first-class snow job. And Andrea was sure she could convince Mercy to see the truth about that. She just had to get her away from Conner Egan long enough to talk some sense into her.

Relieved, Andrea left her hiding place and stepped out onto the path, wondering how long it would take her feet to warm up.

She never knew what hit her.

Out of nowhere, the wind began. It started slowly, a rustle behind her in the trees. Startled, Andrea looked

around. The night had been still and clear. Where had the wind come from? For a moment, it seemed to stop. And then she heard what the wind had masked—the steady sound of something heavy striking the snow behind her. Something was coming along the path. Something enormous. Headed right for her.

The trees began to shake as the wind picked up. It roared through the trees over Andrea's head, sending huge clumps of snow hurtling down all around her. With a shriek, she rushed forward, making a mad dash for the path that cut between the riding rings, out from under the cover of the trees.

She never got that far.

Her foot caught on an unseen obstacle, and she stumbled, crashing face down on the path. She rolled over and scooted backward, her foot still tangled, trying to put some distance between her and whatever was behind her. As abruptly as it began, the wind stopped. The only sound Andrea could hear was her own ragged breathing as she scrambled in the snow, trying desperately to free her feet. And the steady footsteps were coming ever closer.

Then there was silence. Andrea felt like she was in the eye of a storm, in the one moment of quiet before the end of the world. She knew the silence wasn't safe. It was only the prelude to something even more terrible.

The wind returned in full force, screaming through the trees. Then she saw it, coming slowly up the path. And she knew why she hadn't waited to see what was behind her, why she had fled in terror without a second thought.

The thing behind her wasn't human.

The dark shape hovered like smoke above the path. Andrea could just make out enormous arms and legs; hands with horrible, grasping fingers. It had eyes like embers,

glowing red-hot in a face the color of wet ashes. When it saw Andrea, it stopped and parted its lips in a sickening smile, revealing a row of sharp, white teeth. Then it came straight for her.

Andrea gave a final, desperate twist and her legs came free. She rolled backward out of the trees just as the thing came rushing toward her. Andrea could feel its bony fingers wrap around her ankle. With a vicious yank, the thing pulled her backward, dragging her along on her stomach as it sought to haul her back under the cover of the trees. With a scream, Andrea kicked out. She felt her foot connect. The hold on her ankle decreased. She kicked out again, pulling her captured foot forward. And then she was free, scrambling to her feet and running with all her might along the path that led through the outdoor rings to the Riding Academy.

Behind her, she could hear the wind still howling through the trees. And above it, a sound that made her blood run so cold she thought it would never be warm again.

The sound of inhuman laughter.

Conner couldn't remember when he'd laughed so hard. Or when he'd enjoyed his laughter more. It felt good to laugh. To know that he'd frightened Andy Burgess so badly she'd forgotten her fear for Mercy in her fear for herself.

The thought of Andy's concern for Mercy made Conner stop laughing. He'd overlooked Andrea Burgess. His mistake. A mistake he wouldn't make again.

Because nothing was going to interfere with his plans for Mercy. Now that he'd found her, he was determined to

fulfill his dream. The only dream he'd had for over two hundred years.

To claim his final victim in Cooper Hollow. To watch her eyes fill with fear and despair just as his own eyes had. He wanted to bury his teeth in her throat in the same room where his life had ended. He wanted her to know she would be trapped while he was free. Free to live a mortal life where his every wish was granted. While she was doomed to begin her search for a lover to share her fate.

That was the dream that had kept Conner Egan going for over two hundred years. It was the reason he returned to Cooper Hollow, hating every minute he spent there. Every reminder of what he had become.

And if Andrea Burgess got in his way . . . Conner smiled again at the thought of her frantic dash for the Riding Academy.

If Andrea Burgess got in his way, he'd make sure she lived to regret it.

Thirteen

Monday morning always began with an assembly. Ms. Chalmers stood on the podium of the old hotel ballroom, her keen eyes scanning the girls as they filed in to take their seats. The spacious room was usually used for all-school meetings or special presentations. But, in less than a week, it would return to its former glory, transformed for the Valentine Ball.

The Riding Academy students came in quietly. Safe in her seat toward the back of the auditorium, Andrea was doing a little scanning of her own. She was looking for Mercy. She hadn't seen her since Saturday night.

In the cold glare of Sunday morning sunshine, Andrea had felt more than a little foolish about her scare in the woods. In retrospect, it seemed ridiculous to think that she'd really been chased by some supernatural demon. She'd allowed her concerns for Mercedes to run away with her, that was all. It was true her ribs were sore and there were big bruises on her legs. But she'd gotten tangled up. She'd fallen down hard.

Andrea spent Sunday morning in bed and Sunday afternoon working out with Midnight in the indoor ring. The

February horse show was less than a week away. Andrea knew the Riding Academy was counting on her to help them win top honors. She needed to make every practice minute count.

Though Andrea had kept her eyes peeled for Mercy, she'd been unable to spot her all day, and had caught only a glimpse of her at dinner Sunday night. It wasn't unusual for the friends to go a day without seeing much of each other. But Andrea couldn't shake the feeling that Mercy was avoiding her.

Sunday night was the one time they always spent together. Andrea got a letter from home every Saturday, and it had become a tradition that she and Mercy spent Sunday evening catching up on Bill's latest adventure and putting any new pictures into Andy's scrapbook. But last night when Andrea had knocked on Mercy's door, she hadn't answered.

Andrea had seen a band of light under the door, shining out into the darkened hallway. She'd been almost *sure* Mercy was there. The silence from inside the room felt alive; it had a tense, listening quality to it. But short of breaking down the door, there wasn't anything Andrea could do. She'd taken her scrapbook and trudged back to her room, quietly looking at pictures of her family until it was time for lights out.

She'd waited almost half an hour before she'd dared creep back to Mercedes' room. It usually took the group of teachers who watched the halls, nicknamed "The Chalmers Patrol," at least that long to make their rounds and make sure everybody obeyed the curfew. Mercy couldn't possibly have snuck off before then.

But somehow, she had. It had taken the wait for The Chalmers Patrol to make Andrea remember that she had

a way to find out if Mercedes was in her room, even if she didn't answer the door. She and Mercedes had exchanged keys.

Since the attack on the girl in the graveyard, many Riding Academy girls had taken to locking their rooms at night. Andrea knew she ran the risk of frightening her friend if she burst in upon her. But the one sure way to find out if Mercedes had snuck out to meet Conner Egan was for Andrea to go into her room and find out.

The minute Andrea had stepped into Mercedes' room, she'd known her friend wasn't there. The feeling that the room was occupied was gone. Her bed was messy, and her pillows were arranged in a lumpy mass in the middle of the bed, almost as if she'd been trying to fool somebody coming in to look for her.

Andrea had sat for what felt like hours on Mercedes' bed, clutching the bedspread tightly in both hands. Her friend was out there, somewhere in the night, with a guy she'd met only the day before. And a killer was still on the loose somewhere in the neighborhood. She'd put herself in danger and Andrea had failed to stop her.

Silently, Andrea left Mercedes' room and crept back to her own. It was a very long time before she fell asleep.

Fourteen

It was close to curfew on Monday night. In the soft glow of her desk light, Mercedes turned from side to side. She looked at her reflection in the mirror with satisfaction. After several tries at finding the right outfit, she was sure this was just the thing to help Conner forget his old girlfriend.

The soft black dress was something her mother had sent her, convinced that no young lady should be without her basic black and pearls. Mercedes had stuffed it in the back of the closet. She hated wearing black. She thought it made her look like Morticia Addams. But she couldn't stand the thought of not measuring up to Conner's old girlfriend. If the other girl had worn black, then Mercy would, too. It was the perfect way to prove her love, to show Conner she was right for him.

Mercedes smiled at herself in the mirror as she thought about the second part of her plan. She'd lain awake late Sunday night thinking about it. Performers were proud of their dressing rooms. Mercedes knew that from going to the movies. They kept all sorts of personal mementos and good luck charms to guarantee a good performance.

Last night, Mercedes had met Conner outside the Night Owl Club. But tonight, she'd surprise him with something special. She'd bring flowers to his dressing room at the club.

It hadn't been easy to get flowers when she couldn't go into Cooper Hollow. She'd finally convinced Mrs. Alcott, who was going into town to see about arrangements for the ball, to bring her back something from the florist. She'd told Mrs. Alcott the flowers were for Andrea, to encourage her friend to do her best at the horse show.

Touched by Mercedes' thoughtfulness, Mrs. Alcott had agreed to run the errand. At Mercedes' request, she'd brought back an enormous bunch of Oriental lilies. The heavy fragrance of the huge white flowers filled the air of Mercedes' room. She could hardly wait to take them to Conner. She could just imagine how his beautiful green eyes would sparkle with delight and surprise.

"I knew you were special, Mercy," Conner would say to her again. *"There's no one in the world I love as much as you."* And Mercedes would know she had won. All thoughts of his former girlfriend would be banished from Conner's mind. From now on, he would think only of her.

"Lights out!" Mercedes heard the call come down the corridor as The Chalmers Patrol began its evening rounds. Immediately, Mercedes reached out and snapped off her bedroom light. She didn't want to attract any extra attention. It was bad enough that Andrea suspected her.

Mercedes sat down on the bed, impatient for The Chalmers Patrol to leave the area. Andy had been in her room last night. Mercy was sure of it. The bed pillows she'd wadded up had been carefully smoothed out and put back in place.

I'll have to do something about Andrea, Mercedes

thought. She still liked Andy. But their friendship didn't seem so important now that Mercedes had Conner. Having a boyfriend meant that other relationships took second place. Andrea would have to understand that. And if Andy continued to disapprove of Mercy's relationship with Conner, that was just too bad. Mercy wasn't about to let that disapproval interfere with her chance for love.

Nothing could be allowed to do that. Nothing.

The corridor outside was quiet. The Chalmers Patrol had moved on. Mercedes got up from the bed and slipped on her coat. Quietly, she made her way to the dresser and picked up the lilies. They rustled softly in their shiny plastic wrapping. Still moving quietly, she slowly eased open her bedroom door and stepped out into the hall. There was nobody in sight.

To be absolutely safe, she should wait at least fifteen or twenty minutes more, until the patrol had completed its rounds and gone to bed. But the longer she waited, the greater the risk of running into Andy.

Grasping the bunch of lilies tightly in one hand, Mercedes slipped silently along the hallway and peered around the corner. Still, the coast was clear. She was all the way down the back stairs, her hand almost on the door, before Andrea caught up with her.

"Mercy," Andrea said, her sharp whisper cutting through the darkness. She was hiding in the alcove near the back door. Mercedes started and the wrapping on the flowers burst open. The lilies went tumbling to the floor.

"Andrea," Mercedes hissed in dismay. She crouched down, frantically gathering up the spilled blossoms.

"What in the hell do you think you're doing?" Andrea asked. She sounded absolutely furious.

"None of your business," Mercedes replied. She got to

84

her feet, reassembling the bouquet as best she could. Mercedes could feel the prick of tears just behind her eyelids. Andrea was going to ruin everything.

"You're ruining everything, Andy," Mercedes said aloud. "Get out of my way. I'm going out there whether you like it or not."

The door at the top of the stairs opened and both girls immediately fell silent, pulling back into the shelter of the alcove. If they got caught now, both of them were in a lot of trouble.

The member of The Chalmers Patrol responsible for the back stairs listened for a moment from the top of the landing. Mercedes found herself praying the woman wouldn't turn on the light. Finally, the door shut and the sound of footsteps assured the girls that the woman was continuing with her rounds.

Instantly, Mercedes grasped the heavy back door of the Riding Academy and jerked it open. She stepped outside into the snow.

"Mercy, for God's sake," Andrea cried. "I'm your best friend. How can you say that what you're doing is none of my business?" At the sound of the fear and pain in her friend's voice, Mercedes turned around.

"I'm just going to meet Conner for a few hours, Andrea," she said quietly. Conner might mean more to her than Andy did now, but that didn't mean she wanted to abandon her friend. "I'm not spending the night with him or anything."

"It's dangerous out there, Mercy," Andrea hissed. She followed Mercedes outside, keeping one hand on the Riding Academy door. "All sorts of things could happen. You of all people should know that."

Mercedes gave a low laugh. "Nothing's going to happen

to me, Andy," she said. "I was fine last night; I'll be fine tonight. Conner said so." Mercedes could see Andrea take a deep breath, plainly determined to keep on arguing.

"Nothing you can say will make me change my mind," Mercedes said, before Andrea could speak up. "You can either turn me in or get out of my way. But, unless you turn me in, I'm going."

The two girls stared at each other. Mercedes could see Andrea's resolve begin to waver.

"I'll wait up for you," Andrea whispered. "I'll wait in your room until you get back."

"You will not," Mercedes answered forcefully. "What if they do a room check and discover you're not there? Then they'll start checking everybody. Andy," Mercedes said, "if you're really my friend, you'll go back inside and pretend you never saw me."

"That's not fair, Mercy!" Andrea's face was pale and desperate with worry. But Mercedes knew she'd won.

"Don't worry," she whispered. She leaned in to give Andrea a quick, fierce hug. "Be happy for me."

Then she was gone, hurrying down the path that would take her past the stables and the outdoor riding rings. The night air felt wonderful against her face. Even in the cold, Mercedes could smell the heavy scent of the flowers she was carrying.

Soon, Mercy thought. Soon she'd be with Conner. And she'd hear again how much he loved her.

She was unaware of Andrea standing on the back steps of the Riding Academy, watching until she was out of sight.

Fifteen

Monday night was quiet at the Night Owl Club.

Since both the Hudson Military Academy and the Cooper Riding Academy had early weeknight curfews, it was usually just Cooper Hollow High students who came to the club during the week. Of course the students at the private schools didn't always obey the rules. You could see Academy uniforms at the club during the middle of the week. But Monday night was usually pretty dead. It was the night Jake and Jenny Demos spent putting the club back together after the hectic weekend.

Mercedes wished the club were a little busier as she pulled open the outer door and stepped inside. She felt pretty conspicuous. Her down jacket only covered the top part of her black dress. She could see the few students in the club turn to look at her as she came in. But she wasn't going to let her sudden embarrassment stop her. She'd come to see Conner. Nothing else mattered.

There was a young woman behind the snack bar, polishing the counter. She looked nice, her blond hair pulled back from her face in a loose ponytail. Mercedes decided

the woman might know where Conner's dressing room was.

"Hi," Mercedes said, as she approached the counter. The woman looked up in surprise.

"Oh, you startled me," the woman said. "We're just about ready to close. I didn't expect anybody to come in so late." She took the sting out of her words with a quick smile.

"I'm Jenny Demos," the young woman said. Mercedes could see Jenny take in her dress and the bouquet of flowers. A strange, wary expression came over her face.

"Can I help you with something?" she asked.

"I'm looking for Conner Egan, the lead singer from Elysian Fields," Mercedes answered. Jenny Demos didn't say anything. She began to polish the counter again, moving her rag with long, angry swipes.

"I was hoping you could tell me where his dressing room is," Mercedes continued, summoning up her courage. The rag stopped moving and Jenny stared at her.

"His dressing room," she repeated.

"Sure," said Mercedes, trying a smile. She held out the bouquet of flowers. "I wanted to leave these for him," she said. "Aren't they beautiful?"

Jenny Demos seemed at a loss for words. She stared across the counter at Mercedes and fiddled with her polishing cloth. She pulled it through her fingers with quick, hard jerks.

"I'm sorry," she said finally. "I can't tell you where Conner's dressing room is."

Mercedes could hardly believe her ears. She never imagined she'd come this far only to be turned away.

"What do you mean, you can't tell me?" Mercedes

asked. She tried to keep the tears out of her voice. "Don't you know?"

"I'm sorry," Jenny Demos said again, more firmly this time. "I can't tell you where it is."

"I can tell you," a voice behind Mercedes said. She swung around to face one of the strangest looking men she'd ever seen. His white hair stood up in tufts around his deeply-lined face. His sharp nose and burning eyes reminded her of a hawk. He looked just like some fierce bird of prey.

"I can tell you where Conner's room is," the old man repeated.

"Dad," Jenny Demos said sharply. Mercedes turned to look at her. Jenny's face was pale and strained. "You can't do this," Jenny Demos said to her father.

"I can do whatever has to be done," Mr. Demos replied. Mercedes felt like a spectator at a tennis match, her head bouncing back and forth between father and daughter. Their conversation didn't make any sense. What was the big deal about telling her where Conner's dressing room was?

"How can you tell her where that room is?" Jenny Demos asked.

"It's a simple request for information, Jen," Mr. Demos answered. "Not answering the question would be interfering. And you know how I—we—feel about that."

"That's it," Jenny Demos said coldly. "I've heard enough." She threw her towel down on the snack bar and came out from around the counter. Angrily, she brushed past Mercedes and her father on her way to the other room.

"Last call," Jenny cried. "The Night Owl Club is closing for the night."

Mr. Demos watched silently as his daughter moved

through the other rooms, closing down the club. Then he turned back to Mercedes.

"Go upstairs and continue all the way to the end of the hall," the old man said. "Conner's room is the last door you'll come to."

The staircase leading to the second floor was dusty. The higher Mercy climbed, the more dirty her coat got where it brushed against the bannister. The upstairs hallway seemed to go on forever. There were only a few lights in the upper hall, and not all of them worked. The ones that did sent out a feeble light that didn't make it all the way to the floor. Standing at the top of the stairs, Mercedes could just make out the doorway at the far end of the hall. A thin band of light shone under the door.

Conner's room.

It was cold upstairs. *I thought heat was supposed to rise.* Mercedes stared down the long corridor. *How can the downstairs be so nice and the upstairs be so crummy?* Mercedes felt a stab of indignation for Conner's having to work in conditions like this. She became more and more certain that the surprise she had planned was just what he needed.

Gripping the blossoms tightly in one hand, she started forward down the long hallway toward Conner's room.

Conner Egan was feeling good. He was feeling full and powerful. The blood of his last victim still pounded through his veins. It would be a while before he needed to feed again. If he ever did. If all went well, the girl he'd left in the old graveyard would be the last victim Conner

would ever claim as a vampire. By the end of the week, he would be free. Mercedes Amberson would take his place.

At the thought of Mercy, Conner smiled and ran his tongue along the edges of his sharp, white teeth. She was so perfect, Conner thought, as he made his way through the woods toward his room at the Night Owl Club. She'd make a beautiful vampire.

Already, Mercedes loved him so much she'd do anything for him. All he had to do was get her to declare her love. To swear she'd do anything to prove it. Then his vampire existence would be over and hers would begin.

Conner stopped for a moment to think about what would happen then. When he was no longer a vampire. He'd have a mortal life filled with whatever he wanted. For as long as he lived.

He wondered suddenly what Julia McKenzie had done with what was left of her life. He knew what he'd do with his. The girl in the graveyard wouldn't be the last to die. Oh, no. He'd make sure people paid for what had happened to him. As many as it took to quench his rage. A rage that had not left him in over two hundred years.

The rage had been his enemy at first. So great he hadn't even bothered to appear in human form. For nearly a hundred years he'd been little more than an animal. Viciously draining the blood of his victims and nursing his hatred of what he'd become. Only gradually had Conner realized that his rage kept him from achieving his freedom. And so he'd learned to conquer it. The rage had never left him. But now it flowed, just beneath the surface, fast and deadly.

Conner stretched. It was time to go back inside. The blue light above the door to the Night Owl Club was off when Conner came around the corner. The club was

closed. But he could hear loud voices coming from inside. Grinning, he decided to go in through the main door. That way he could catch a glimpse of his employers.

Conner hated Jake and Jenny Demos. Hated them for their passivity, their pledge of non-interference. It wasn't that he wanted them to try and stop him. But you had to take a stand. You had to take action. Claiming you had the right to do nothing just gave you an excuse to say "it wasn't my fault" when something went wrong.

He opened the door and walked straight into the middle of their argument.

Jenny Demos stopped talking the moment Conner stepped into the room. Her cheeks were flushed with anger. Her entire body quivered with emotion. Conner enjoyed tormenting Jenny. He knew that in spite of her vow of non-interference it bothered her that she couldn't stop him. Bothered her that he'd claim his final victim upstairs at her club.

"Good evening, Jenny," Conner said smoothly. He nodded in the general direction of her father. "Mr. Demos," he said.

"Go peddle it somewhere else, Conner Egan," Jenny Demos snapped. "Nobody here is buying your smooth talk. We know what you are."

Conner smiled at her. "It's a good thing not everyone has your perspective," he answered. A tense silence filled the room. Jenny glanced quickly at her father and then looked away.

What have they been arguing about? Conner wondered suddenly. He had the distinct feeling it had to do with him.

"Like Mercedes Amberson," Conner continued. Jenny Demos' face slowly turned an ugly red. Conner watched

her clench and unclench her fists. He was delighted with Jenny's reaction.

That's it, he thought. *They've been arguing about Mercy.*

"Mercy Amberson thinks she's in love with me," Conner went on. He looked at Jenny and smiled. "And you know what that means," he said.

"It means she doesn't know you," Jake Demos answered. "I wonder what would happen if she did?"

"She'll know me soon enough," Conner replied, stung to hear Jake Demos speak up. Conner had no doubt the old man hated him just as much as his daughter did. But, until now, he'd kept strictly out of Conner's way. "But by then it will be too late, won't it?" Conner taunted him.

"I wouldn't be too sure about that," Jenny Demos said. Again, she made quick eye contact with her father. A strange feeling came over Conner. The Demoses weren't actually *doing* anything, but, standing between them, Conner began to feel as if he were slowly being trapped.

"She might find out about you in a way you can't predict," Jenny continued. Conner felt his heart begin to pound in heavy strokes inside his chest.

They know something, he thought. *Something dangerous to me.*

And then he heard it. Slow and steady, the sound of footsteps overhead. He jerked his head back, listening intently.

Where is it coming from? he wondered. And then he was running, taking the stairs two at a time in his haste to reach the second story.

The sound was coming from his room.

Sixteen

Mercedes thought Conner's room was beautiful. She would never have guessed it would be so nice after the ugliness of the dusty hall.

The room was surprisingly simple and old fashioned. An old dresser and writing table stood together at the far end. The room was hot. Mercedes shrugged out of her coat and placed it gently on the antique quilt spread across the four poster bed. Just for a moment, as she touched the soft, old fabric, Mercedes thought she was touching her own quilt. The one Granny Amberson had made, the one that she kept on her bed at the Riding Academy.

Surprised, Mercedes jerked her hand back. Instantly, the illusion was gone.

Dream on, Amberson, she told herself as she stepped away from the bed. *I wonder what my therapist would make of that one?*

Turning to survey the rest of the room, she spotted where she wanted to put the flowers immediately.

Resting on the old dresser was a pale blue pitcher. It even had water in it. Mercedes carefully arranged the flowers and then stood back to admire the effect. Already, the

thick scent of the lilies filled the air. Beyond the flowers, she could see her own reflection in the wavy surface of the old dresser's mirror. The lilies glowed against the black fabric of her dress.

How beautiful, she thought dreamily, as she watched the two reflections ripple in the old mirror. The sweet air of the room reached out and embraced her. Mercedes felt warm and happy. Everything was just perfect.

It didn't stay that way for long.

The door of the room flew open with incredible force, crashing against the wall and bouncing back. With a cry of surprise, Mercedes spun around. Conner Egan stood in the doorway. But this Conner was unlike anything Mercedes had ever seen before.

His breath came in huge gasps. His eyes were wild and furious. Without warning, he lunged across the room, grabbing Mercedes' arm and jerking her away from the dresser.

"What the hell do you think you're doing here?" he asked, pulling her into the center of the room.

Mercedes was startled and frightened. Conner's tight grip on her arm hurt.

"I brought you some flowers," she stammered. "I wanted to surprise you."

"Surprise me," Conner repeated. *"Surprise* me." Now he held her by both elbows and swung her around, forcing her to look up at him.

Gone was the beautiful hero of Mercedes' dreams. Conner's lips were a thin white line of anger. He looked ugly and mean. She felt as if she were looking at a stranger.

"Let me show you how I feel about surprises, Mercy," Conner told her. He squeezed her elbows until she squirmed in pain. Whimpering, she tried to pull away. Con-

ner released her elbows suddenly and made a grab for her long dark hair. Stumbling, she clutched at his knees trying to keep her balance.

"I don't like surprises," Conner said. He jerked her head from side to side as he spoke, and Mercedes started to cry. She didn't mean to. But she couldn't seem to stop the huge, hot tears from running down her cheeks.

"And I don't like crybabies. Now I want you to apologize," Conner said softly. "You want to apologize, don't you, Mercy?" Terrified, she nodded. "You don't want me to be angry, do you?" This time, she shook her head. She was telling the truth.

"Then tell me that you're sorry," Conner said. "Say, 'Conner, I'm sorry I came to your room without permission. I won't ever do it again.' "

He tightened his grip on her hair. "Say it, Mercy," he said.

Mercedes took a huge, quavering breath. She'd never be able to make it through the apology, she thought desperately. She knew she wouldn't.

Conner's grip was so tight the skin on Mercedes' face felt stretched. She'd never make it through the apology without crying. And then what would he do?

"I'm waiting, Mercy," Conner said.

"Conner," she began. "Conner, I'm—" But the sound of her voice saying his name undid her. Once again, the tears began to stream down her face. She watched as Conner Egan's face grew unrecognizable with fury.

This isn't Conner, Mercedes thought, as she watched him raise his arm. Just like in the graveyard, everything was weird and hazy . . . *Not the Conner I was so sure I loved* . . .

And then her entire head exploded with pain as Conner brought the back of his hand down across her face.

The second Mercedes hit the floor, Conner realized his mistake.

She lay there, quivering and trying not to sob. Trying not to cry so he would have no reason to hit her again.

My God, Conner Egan thought. The rage drained out of him, and his entire body turned cold. *What have I just done?*

She'd been in his room. The source of his power. She couldn't be allowed to enter it too soon. Her coming here could have ruined everything. And if her arrival hadn't, his reaction probably had.

I've got to keep her, Conner thought desperately. *I'm too close to lose her now.*

"Mercy," he cried, falling to his knees beside her. "Oh, God, baby, I'm so sorry." He knelt on the floor and took Mercedes gently into his arms. She resisted just for a moment, looking up at him with enormous, frightened eyes.

Her face was swollen from crying and the slap he'd given her. Slowly, gently, Conner reached out to touch the place where his hand had struck her. He watched as she tried not to flinch.

"I didn't mean to hurt you, sweetheart," he said softly. He let his beautiful green eyes fill slowly with regret. "I'd never hurt you. I love you," he whispered.

Mercedes began to sob in earnest, burying her face against his chest.

He rocked her from side to side and stroked her hair.

"Mercy, honey, I'm so sorry. I didn't mean to hurt you,"

Conner said again. "You know that don't you?" he asked her. He could feel her head nod beneath his hand.

"It'll never happen again, Mercy," Conner said. He continued to rock her and gently stroke her head. "I promise, sweetheart. I'm so sorry. It will never happen again."

Mercedes' sobs began to subside. Her uneven breathing was the only sign she'd been upset.

"I had to do it, Mercy," Conner said. "You understand that, don't you?" She was still and quiet in his arms. "You did something we hadn't agreed on," Conner said patiently.

"My privacy is very important to me," Conner went on. "We agreed to meet outside. We never agreed you could come up here.

"You broke our agreement," Conner continued gently. "And I had to make sure you knew not to do that. Ever again." He shifted her in his arms so that he could look down into her tear stained face. "You understand that, don't you sweetheart?" he asked.

Mercedes' huge, dark eyes looked up at him. Conner could feel her indecision. Feel her love battling with her fear. He was close, but he hadn't won her back yet.

Do something, his mind screamed. *Do something. You're losing her.* Gently, he reached down to stroke her face.

"I wanted to invite you to come up here, Mercy," he said softly. "I wanted it to be special." He leaned down and gently kissed her hurt cheek. He felt Mercy quiver and catch her breath.

"I love you, Mercy," Conner said. "I need you. I only got so mad because I thought I wasn't going to be able to do something special with you.

"Give me another chance," Conner said, his voice vibrating with emotion. "A chance to prove my love. Please, Mercy. Please."

For what seemed like a lifetime, Conner held his breath. Then, slowly, hesitantly, she nodded her head. Conner smiled a tender smile and leaned down to kiss her lips. It was a long, slow kiss. And Conner filled it with all his desire for her. All his desire for his own freedom. By the time the kiss was over, he knew she belonged to him once more.

"You won't regret it," he promised, smiling down at her. "I'll make you so happy, you'll forget this ever happened."

A ghost of a smile appeared on Mercedes' face. "Forget what happened, Conner?" she asked. Conner laughed and held her close.

"You know what I'd like?" he said softly. "I'd like us to do something really romantic. Just the two of us." He kept his voice gentle and his movements slow. He leaned down to kiss her other cheek and the tip of her nose.

"You'd like that, too, wouldn't you?" he asked. Before she could answer, he spoke again. "Please, sweetheart," Conner begged. "Let me make it up to you."

Mercedes lay still in his arms and gazed up at him, her face pale but happy.

"What do you want to do, Conner?" she asked.

"You know there's a lake in the woods?" Conner asked, brushing a few strands of hair back from her face.

"Um hm," she murmured.

"It's really beautiful this time of year," Conner said. "It freezes solid and you can walk all the way across it. And on the far side is a little glen, just perfect for a late-night picnic."

Mercedes looked at him as if he'd gone a little crazy.

"Conner, it's winter," she said. "How can we have a picnic in the middle of the night in the snow?"

"That's my secret, Mercy," Conner answered. "Just

think of it," he went on. He began to rock gently back and forth, cradling her as if she were a small child. Lulling her with his quiet voice.

"The moon will be almost full," Conner said. "The lake will sparkle in the moonlight. It'll be just the two of us, Mercy. The two of us in the moonlight."

"Doesn't that sound romantic?" he asked. She nodded. Her eyes as she looked up at him were shiny and full of love.

"Close your eyes," Conner whispered. "Close your eyes and imagine us there together." Conner bent his head and ran soft kisses up her neck.

"We'll ride through the woods on horseback, just like we're in some old movie," Conner murmured. "Then I'll carry you across the ice to our special place on the far side of the lake." He paused for a moment.

"You'd like us to be there together, wouldn't you, Mercy?" he asked softly.

"Yes," she whispered, her eyes shut tight.

"You can get a horse can't you? Nobody will know."

"Nobody will know," she repeated after him.

"Look at me, Mercy," Conner breathed. Opening her eyes, she looked at him with a dreamy expression, like she was in a trance—entirely powerless in the grip of her love, of her desire to be with him.

"Will you meet me?" he asked softly. He kissed her eyelids closed again.

"Yes," Mercedes whispered again. "Yes."

"You're not worried about taking your horse from the Riding Academy?"

"I can do it, Conner," she said earnestly. "I know I can."

Conner smiled. "I know you can, too, Mercy," he said.

100

Then, very tenderly, he took her neck into his mouth and sank his teeth into her throat.

It was dangerous to take her blood. He knew that. But he couldn't seem to help himself. The longing to taste her was simply too great.

Just a little, he promised himself, as the sweet red fluid began to fill his mouth. Just enough to know what she tasted like.

No more bright ideas, my angel of Mercy, Conner thought, tightening his grip. *From now on, I'll keep you docile and quiet.* Mercy whimpered softly and then lay still. Her eyes still closed, she had no idea what was happening.

Conner intended to see things stayed that way.

He'd have no more scares like the one he'd had tonight. Taking her blood was a calculated risk. Too much and he'd interfere with her ability to say she loved him genuinely, without his will being imposed on hers. But he couldn't afford any more surprises. The last one had almost cost him everything.

And, God, she tasted sweet. So incredibly sweet. Removing himself gently from her throat, Conner placed his lips over the teeth marks, sucking down the last few drops of blood.

You're mine, Mercy Amberson, he thought. The sweet taste of her blood lingered in the back of his throat.

Before the week is out, you'll be looking for someone to love you forever. And I'll be looking at my freedom.

Seventeen

"Looking good, Andrea!"

Mercedes sat in the stands of the indoor riding ring and cheered Andrea on as she put Midnight through his paces. Girls competing in the February horse show had been given extra riding time throughout the week. It was Wednesday, and the competition was on Saturday, just three days away.

Technically, Mercedes wasn't supposed to be in the ring with Andrea. But she'd made sure her regular riding session was scheduled for the same time as Andrea's extra practice session. Then she'd pleaded a headache and asked to be excused. Ms. Saberhagen didn't really care whether or not Mercedes took her usual riding time. She'd long since abandoned any hope of Mercedes' ever being more than just a barely competent horsewoman.

Mercedes rubbed her hand across her eyes and wished that her headache had only been a convenient excuse. She hadn't really felt well since the night she'd gone to take flowers to Conner's dressing room. Her head throbbed; her throat felt raw and sore. She was almost glad that Conner had suggested they cool things down for a few days. It

gave her a chance to rest. And to spend some time with Andrea.

Andy really was a superb rider, Mercedes thought as she watched her friend maneuver around the ring. And she looked great on Midnight. Her fair hair and pale complexion made a startling contrast to the jet black coat and mane of the horse. She looked like an elf plunked down on a warrior's charger by mistake. Andrea finished cantering Midnight around the ring and stopped in front of Mercy.

"Hey, Merce," Andrea said, sliding to the ground. "Help me with the cavaletti, will you?"

Mercedes stood up and walked down the bleachers to the floor of the riding arena. Together, she and Andrea wrestled the first of the obstacles into position. Midnight was long past the point where he needed the cavaletti bars to show him what to do. But they were a good way of keeping both horse and rider in good condition. Jumping was Andrea's strongest event.

The two girls worked their way around the ring in silence. Mercy could see that Andy was feeling better. Her face was relaxed and she'd stopped watching Mercy out of the corner of her eye, as if she expected her to disappear at any instant.

It's working, Mercedes thought, as she and Andrea dragged the last bar into position. *She doesn't suspect a thing.*

Since their confrontation at the back door of the Riding Academy two nights ago, Mercedes had been spending almost all of her free time with Andrea. This was the second afternoon she'd watched her friend practice for the horse show. And they'd spent Tuesday evening together, reading over Andy's latest letter from home and pasting a whole batch of new pictures into the scrapbook. Neither

...ioned the fact that Mercy hadn't been around to ...rform this weekly ritual on Sunday.

Mercedes hadn't actually said that she and Conner had broken up, but she could tell that Andrea thought they had. That assumption was just fine with Mercedes. It meant Andrea wouldn't be following her around anymore.

"Totally gross," Andrea said, taking a big, white handkerchief from the pocket of her riding jacket and wiping her face.

"Girls of the Cooper Hollow Riding Academy do not say things like 'totally gross' Andrea Burgess," Mercedes said, suppressing a laugh. "And I would like to remind you that we do not *sweat.*"

"I know, I know," Andrea groaned. "We perspire. And I think I'm doing more than my fair share."

She snapped Mercedes with the handkerchief and then stuffed it back into her pocket. Together, the two girls walked back to where Midnight waited patiently on the side of the ring.

"Mercy," Andrea said quietly. Mercedes looked over at her friend.

"Thanks for coming to watch me practice again today," Andrea said.

Mercedes smiled. "You're welcome."

"Got any plans for tonight?" Andrea asked as she swung herself up into the saddle, her voice friendly and neutral.

You don't fool me, Andrea, Mercedes thought. *I know what you're really asking.*

"I have some studying I need to do," Mercedes said as she started up the bleachers. She was glad her back was turned so that Andy couldn't see her face. Mercedes had never been very good at lying. Her face always gave her

away. "I'm a little behind," she continued, bending and rummaging in her shoulder bag.

Andrea was silent for a moment, fidgeting with Midnight's harness. "Need any help?" she finally asked.

"I don't think so," Mercedes answered as nonchalantly as she could. She wished she didn't feel so *guilty* about lying to Andrea.

It's the only way, Mercedes reminded herself. Andrea mustn't suspect that she was taking her horse to meet Conner later that night. Andrea had to think Mercedes was staying home, safe in her room at the Riding Academy.

"I'll probably be going back and forth between my room and the library," Mercedes continued. "You'd never get any studying of your own done."

Andrea continued to fidget. "Mercy," she finally said. Mercedes knew what was coming next.

"I don't want to talk about it, Andrea," she said turning around quickly. "Just because you're my friend doesn't mean you have the right to question me all the time."

One look at Andrea's hurt face made Mercedes wish she hadn't come down quite so hard on her friend.

It's the only way, Mercedes told herself again. She couldn't take the chance of confiding in her. If Andrea knew Conner had hit her, she'd go through the roof. Mercedes believed Conner when he said he would never hit her again. And she was determined to give him a second chance.

"Come on, Andy," she said as brightly as she could. "I came here to cheer you on, not to argue with you."

She assumed "the Ms. Chalmers position" on the bleachers, sitting stiffly, her spine ramrod straight. "Now remember, young lady," Mercy said. "There are only three

105

more practice days left until the Big Event. And I expect to see some first class jumps out of you."

Andrea gave Mercedes a wan smile.

"Yes, ma'am," she said, turning Midnight around and heading toward the start of her run.

As she watched Andrea perform a flawless series of jumps, Mercedes settled back on the bleachers and sneaked a peek at her watch. It was only three o'clock. She couldn't meet Conner for hours yet. Mercy sighed and concentrated on watching Andrea's progress around the ring.

It was going to be a very long afternoon.

Mercedes had never been in the stable at night before. In the dark, it was an entirely different world. The horses' heads looming out at her from the shadows looked enormous. The light of her flashlight glinted off dark, glassy eyes. Everywhere, there were strange sounds: The heavy thud of hooves against stall floors; huge, gusty sighs of breath. Mercedes felt as if the entire building were alive. Alive and watching her.

The stable was equipped with powerful worklights, but Mercedes couldn't turn them on. She was afraid someone from one of the other Academy buildings would notice. The flashlight she'd filched from the utility closet by the Academy back door wasn't very powerful, but it was better than nothing.

Cautiously watching the tiny ring of light on the floor, she made her way down the row of stalls to where her own horse was stabled. She could feel her heart pounding in nervous anticipation. She'd waited two long days for this

date with Conner. She could hardly wait for the evening to really begin.

Abruptly, her foot snagged on the uneven surface of the floor. The flashlight went flying as she put her hands out to brace herself. It landed with a metallic thud. She could see the light waver, and then go out.

Great, Mercedes thought. *With my luck, it's probably broken.* She crawled slowly in the direction of where she'd last seen the light. Her hand was on the flashlight and she was starting to rise when something grabbed the top of her head.

Stifling a shriek, Mercedes fell backward. She shook the flashlight violently, rattling the batteries inside. It worked. A pale light shone upward, directly onto the name on the door of the closest stall.

Mercedes set the flashlight down on the floor of the stable and buried her face in her hands. She didn't know whether to laugh or cry. The flying flashlight had rolled up to the stall marked "Amber." Recognizing Mercedes even in the darkness, Amber had reached down and softly lipped the top of Mercedes' head.

She'd been frightened by her own horse.

Snatching up the flashlight, Mercedes scrambled to her feet and headed for Amber's stall. She'd wasted enough time. She had to saddle the horse and meet Conner.

Andrea rummaged among the papers on her desk. Where was her reporter's notebook? She'd promised herself that this was the night she'd finish the article about Elysian Fields for the Riding Academy newspaper.

She'd put off the story for as long as she could because of her concern over Mercedes' relationship with Conner.

But she couldn't put it off any longer. The band was popular; they were hot; and she'd already told Jenny Demos and half the school she was doing a story on them. She had to carry out her assignment. But she couldn't find her notes or the band's press packet anywhere. What had she *done* with them?

And then she'd remembered. She'd taken extra time rubbing down Midnight after their riding session. Midnight had worked hard that afternoon, and Andrea had wanted to make sure the horse felt appreciated and well cared for. She'd had to dash to make it back to the main building in time to get cleaned up for dinner. In her hurry, she'd accidentally dumped the contents of her shoulder bag on the floor of Midnight's stall. She must not have retrieved everything; the notebook must still be there.

Andrea sat still for a moment, weighing her options. She knew that since the murder it was forbidden to go outside alone after dark. She ought to get a partner to go with her to the stables. But if Andrea went to find Mercy now, Mercy probably would accuse her of spying. Of trying to figure out if she was planning to sneak off to meet Conner.

Groaning, Andrea pulled herself up from her desk chair and grabbed her coat from the closet. If she wanted to get that story off her back, she had no choice but to go out to the stables alone and get that notebook.

Except for the incident with the flashlight, everything was going flawlessly. Mercedes was surprised at how easy it was to saddle Amber in the dark. Amber was one of the most placid horses at the Riding Academy, her temperament ideally suited to the skills of her rider. She'd been

more than happy to stand patiently while Mercedes saddled her up and lead her down the length of the stable in the dark.

Mercedes brought the horse to a standstill just inside the stable exit. Slowly, she eased back the big sliding door. This was the most dangerous part of the whole evening. In the stall, she could have made up some excuse, some reason for coming to see Amber after hours. But standing next to the stable door with her horse saddled could only mean Mercy was planning to break every Riding Academy rule in the book. If she were caught now, everything was over.

Plastered against the side of the building, Mercedes listened intently. A car revved its engine out on Cross Road. The power generator that supplied heat to the stable whined softly. But those were the only sounds she could hear. The snowy night was crystal clear. And silent.

Satisfied, she eased the door back farther, and led Amber out through the opening. Then she slid the huge door shut, grateful that the Riding Academy always kept the door in perfect working order. She wondered what Ms. Chalmers would do if she knew her well cared for equipment had helped Mercedes make good her escape.

"Come on, Amber. Come on, girl," Mercedes whispered. The blood was singing in her ears. Holding Amber's lead tightly in her hand, she guided the horse around the side of the building. With the stable between her and the main Riding Academy buildings, she'd be fine, Mercedes told herself. Then it was just a quick trip through the graveyard and—

A shape materialized in the darkness in front of her. Startled, she cried out and Amber reared up, her front hooves coming all the way off the ground. Mercedes spun

around to face her horse and backed up, pulling down hard on Amber's lead.

"Whoa, Amber," she hissed fiercely in the darkness. "Whoa, Amber. Whoa." The horse resisted, then gave in. She brought her hooves back down with a heavy thud, just inches from Mercedes' feet. Mercy leaned forward to pat Amber's neck, steadying the horse by making physical contact. After a few seconds, Amber relaxed completely. Her hairy lips reached out to nip at the buttons on Mercedes' coat.

Mercedes' heart was pounding so hard she was afraid she'd be sick. She'd been caught! In spite of all her precautions, she'd been caught. She took a deep, shaky breath, and turned to face the person who'd appeared so suddenly in front of her.

It was Andrea.

Mercy released her breath with a sudden whoosh. Her incredible fear turned to anger as she faced her friend. How *dare* Andrea come sneaking after her in the middle of the night? Before Andrea could even open her mouth to speak, Mercedes was on the offensive.

"What are you doing here, Andrea?" she said. Her anger was plain in every line of her body.

"I might ask you the same question, Mercy," Andrea shot back. "I came to get a notebook I'd left in Midnight's stall. I don't think your excuse is quite so good."

"I don't need an excuse," Mercedes said. "I don't care who knows what I'm doing, and I don't care about the consequences. I'm going to meet Conner, and you can't stop me."

"Mercy, for God's sake," Andrea cried.

"You're always saying that, Andrea," Mercedes broke in. "You're always saying, 'Mercy for God's sake.' For

God's sake *what*, Andy?" Mercedes asked, her voice hard. "What do you want me to do? Give up my boyfriend? Give up my chance to see him because of some stupid Riding Academy rule? I don't think so."

"Mercy," Andrea whispered. Her eyes were hurt and frightened. "Mercy, what's the matter with you?"

"Nothing's the matter with me," she snapped. "Except you. Except the fact that you're always following me around and prying into my private life. What I do with Conner is *my* business, not yours. So why don't you just butt out?"

"It is *so* my business," Andrea cried, growing angry in her turn. "I'm your best friend, Mercy. That *makes* it my business."

"Some best friend," Mercedes answered. "Sneaking around behind my back."

"Oh, and you're so much better?" Andrea asked. "Pretending to be interested in watching me practice for the horse show. It was just a lie, wasn't it?" Mercedes could hear the tears just behind the anger in Andrea's voice.

"All you wanted to do was make me think you'd stopped seeing Conner so you could jump on your house and ride off to meet him the minute my back was turned," Andrea continued. "You used me. You don't care about me. *You're* the one who's a lousy friend."

She stopped talking, breathing hard. The two girls stared at each other in the pale moonlight.

"I'm not discussing this any more, Andy," Mercedes said. She wished Andy's words weren't quite so close to the truth. Mercedes gave Amber's lead a tug and tried to maneuver past her friend.

"I'm going, and you can't stop me."

"Mercy," Andrea said. She reached out and pushed on

Amber's neck, forcing the horse to stop. "A week ago you found a dead girl. You thought she talked to you. You were so freaked out, you didn't come out of your room for five whole days. That girl's killer is still out there. Don't you get it? Her killer could be anywhere and you're sneaking off at every opportunity to see some guy you know absolutely nothing about.

"Why can't you see that he's just using you?" Andrea asked. "It's dangerous for you to be out here alone. If Conner really cared about you, he'd never make you do something that put you in danger."

"He's not using me," Mercedes cried. "Conner loves me. He says so. I'm in classes all day. Night is the only time we can be together. What do you want me to do? Invite him to watch TV at the Riding Academy?"

"Mercy," Andrea said again. "If he wants you to do something dangerous, he can't really love you."

"You're just jealous, Andrea," Mercedes said. "You've never liked Conner. You've been jealous of him from the very start."

"That's not *true*," Andrea said.

"It is so true," Mercedes interrupted her. "You don't want me to be happy and have a boyfriend. You want things to be the way they've always been. Poor little rich girl Mercedes being comforted by generous, warm-hearted Andrea. You want me to be content just pasting some stupid family pictures in your scrapbook. Well if that's your idea of friendship, you can keep it.

"I have Conner now," Mercedes said. "He says he loves me, and I believe him. His love is enough for me." Mercedes jerked Amber out of Andrea's hands, and the horse started forward. "I don't need your jealousy," Mercy said over her shoulder. "I don't need *you*."

"And I don't need your lies and accusations," Andrea answered. "Or your warped excuses. If you don't want my friendship, that's fine with me."

"Good," Mercedes said. She turned around to face Andrea. "From now on you can just stay away from me. As of this moment, our friendship is officially over."

without a doubt went wrong in the trailer. She . . . .

Eighteen

"I won't think about it," Mercedes said, as she guided her horse through the Riding Academy graveyard. She didn't realize she'd spoken aloud until she saw Amber prick her ears forward in surprise. Mercedes gave a shaky laugh and reached up to stroke the horse's neck.

"It's all right, girl," Mercedes said soothingly. "We're almost there." And they were. They just had to make it through the old graveyard first.

Damn you, Andrea, Mercedes thought as she maneuvered Amber through the sharp, crooked stones. The idea of going through the graveyard hadn't bothered her until Andrea had mentioned the dead girl. In the incredible glow of her love for Conner, Mercy almost had forgotten the grisly incident of the week before. But now, plodding along the twisted path between the headstones, everything came rushing back.

"I won't think about it," Mercedes said again, consciously speaking aloud this time. "I won't." The sound of her voice helped to take away her fear. Up ahead, she could see the place where the path left the graveyard and entered the Cooper Hollow woods. She knew Conner was

waiting for her, somewhere in the trees. She tried not to think about what might be waiting for her when she returned to the Riding Academy.

Anything is worth being with Conner, Mercy thought. *Anything.* She didn't believe a word of Andrea's accusations. Her assertions that Conner didn't really love Mercy. She *knew* Conner loved her. The fact that he was coming here tonight was proof that he did.

With a sigh of relief, Mercedes led Amber through the last of the headstones and under the trees. All around her, the branches seemed to reach out to welcome her. She moved through them as if she were in a dream. A beautiful dream that would end in Conner's arms.

"Mercy." The sound of his voice was all around her. Mercedes stopped, but she couldn't see Conner. Beside her, Amber arched her neck and whickered softly.

"Mercy," his voice said again.

"I can't find you," Mercedes called. "Where are you?"

"Keep coming, my angel of Mercy," the voice answered. "You'll find me soon enough."

And suddenly he was there. Standing before her on the path in a huge cloak the color of the night sky overhead. His pale features looked like polished marble in the moonlight. When he saw her, Conner smiled.

"Come here, angel of Mercy," he said. "I've been waiting for you."

Mercedes let go of Amber's lead and rushed forward into Conner's arms. He opened the cloak and spread it wide around her, engulfing her in its dark warmth. They kissed until she was breathless.

"You came," he murmured, staring down at her.

"Were you afraid I wouldn't?" she asked with a smile. Her heart kicked into high gear. He had been afraid she

wouldn't show up. He wanted her as much as she wanted him.

"I'm always afraid when you're not with me," Conner murmured against her hair. "Afraid something will stop us from being together."

"Nothing is going to do that, Conner," she said in a quiet voice.

"Oh, God, Mercy," Conner said. His voice was heavy and sweet. "I love you so much," he whispered.

He kissed her again. Mercedes thought she would go crazy if he stopped.

"I love you, too, Conner," she said, when she could finally speak. Conner smiled down at her. The look of joy on his face was like nothing Mercedes had ever seen before.

"I have something for you," Conner said. In one hand, he held an oblong jeweler's box. He handed it to Mercedes. "Open it," he said.

"Now?" she asked.

"Now," he replied. "If you open it now, I'll know that you've really forgiven me."

With trembling fingers, she opened the box. Nestled inside was a beautiful, heart-shaped locket of polished gold.

"Oh, Conner," she breathed. "It's beautiful."

"Do you like it, Mercy?" Conner asked. "Do you really?"

"Are you crazy?" she laughed. "Of course I do."

"Will you wear it for me always?"

"Always," she promised. "Help me put it on." In another moment, she felt the smooth, cold metal of the chain as Conner fastened the pendant around her throat. He pressed

116

his lips against the clasp where it rested at the nape of her neck. Mercedes shivered.

"Are you ready for the rest of your surprise?" Conner asked softly.

Mercedes nodded and, instantly, Conner scooped her up into his arms. He carried her to Amber and, with one fluid motion, set her up on the horse. Then he mounted behind her, settling her firmly back against him and covering her again with his cloak. Mercedes could feel his heart beat deep inside his chest.

Conner made a clicking sound with his tongue, and Amber started forward. They were on their way to the lake.

The lake exceeded Mercedes' wildest dreams. It was vast and still in the moonlight. Its surface glittered with a thousand tiny patterns imbedded deep in the ice. The rising moon was close to full. Even now, it was almost as bright as day.

They left Amber on the shore. Conner spread a thick blanket over the horse to help keep her warm. Then he carried Mercedes to the far side of the lake.

"Close your eyes, Mercy," Conner murmured as they neared the far shore. "Don't open them until I say so."

Laughing, she complied. With her eyes closed, she was entirely dependent on Conner. She could hear the sound of his feet as they left the smooth surface of the ice and crunched through the snow. His powerful legs pumped forward in a steady rhythm. Then she felt him lift her, as if over some obstacle, and set her on her own feet in the snow. He turned her so that her back rested against him.

"You can open your eyes now," Conner said.

She did. And knew that nothing in her life would ever be the same again.

The glen was beautiful. A tiny hollow scooped out of the woods. Huge trees hung over it, protecting it from outside eyes. In the very center was an old sleigh, piled high with sheepskin blankets. And covering everything, their color bright against the snow, were red rose petals. Hundreds and hundreds of them.

It was the most romantic sight Mercedes had ever seen. And Conner had created it just for her.

"Oh, Conner," she breathed, hardly able to trust her voice. "It's so beautiful."

"I'm glad you like it," Conner said softly.

"But where did it come from?" she asked, turning to face him. "How did it all get here?"

"The sleigh was here," Conner admitted. He stepped over the low barrier of shrubs blocking the entrance to the glen and stood next to Mercedes. "It must have been abandoned." He smiled down at her delighted face. "All I did was clean it up and embellish it a little," he said modestly.

Mercedes laughed. "Oh, is that all," she said. Her voice was warm and teasing.

"Well," Conner said. "I did think about it a lot," he continued. He pulled her back into his arms and gave her a long, slow kiss. "Every time I thought of you," he said. "Come on. Let's get you bundled into the sleigh. I don't want you to catch cold."

Catch cold, Mercedes thought as she let him lead her forward. *I'm more likely to melt.* Conner's kisses made her feel like she was on fire.

Mercedes shed her coat and climbed into the old sleigh. Conner pulled the sheepskins up around her. With a flourish, he removed his cloak and spread it over everything.

Then he reached down into the snow beside the sleigh and produced a bottle of champagne.

"May I tempt you with a little champagne, Ms. Amberson?" Conner asked.

Mercedes laughed. "Absolutely, Mr. Egan," she replied.

Conner produced two glasses and popped the cork on the champagne bottle. A moment later, they were toasting one another, like newlyweds at their wedding.

She wished the night would never end. She knew now that she'd been right to trust Conner. To give him another chance. The champagne burned going down her throat and settled warmly in her veins. Conner's kisses were hot against her lips, her ears, and throat.

This is what it feels like to be wanted, Mercy thought. *This is what it feels like to be loved.* Finally, dizzy with wine and excitement, she drew back a little and rested against the far side of the sleigh. She looked at Conner Egan.

His pale skin was flushed against his white shirt. His strange green eyes flickered in the moonlight. Again, Mercedes was reminded of drawings of heroes of the Revolutionary War. The midnight ride of Paul Revere.

I love you, Conner Egan, Mercy thought. *You're everything I ever dreamed of. And you love me.*

Conner smiled. "What are you thinking about?" he asked.

"You," she answered. One of Conner's hands rested near her on the sheepskin, and Mercedes reached out with gentle fingertips to stroke it. She wasn't afraid to show her love anymore.

"Conner," Mercedes said.

"Mmm," Conner answered. He leaned forward and captured her hand, brushing it back and forth against his lips.

"If I wanted us to do something special together, something I'd planned, would that be all right?" she asked. Conner put Mercedes' hand back down on the coverlet and looked at her.

"What do you mean?" he asked.

"Well," she paused. What if he thought going to the Valentine Ball was stupid? she thought suddenly. What if he got angry with her for even suggesting it?

"Well," Conner repeated, prompting her. Mercedes continued in a rush.

"There's a big dance at school after the horse show this Saturday," she said. "A Valentine Ball. The Riding Academy has been doing it for years, and it's a really big deal. I never thought I'd go to the Valentine Ball," Mercedes said in a low voice. "I never thought there'd be anybody I'd want to go with." She looked up at him. "Or who'd want to go with me. Will you go with me, Conner?" she asked. Her voice was just above a whisper.

"A Valentine Ball," Conner repeated. "This Saturday?"

She nodded. "I know it's really short notice," she began. "And it isn't really on Valentine's Day. It's on the thirteenth. But that's the only day the school could have it."

"None of that matters, Mercy," Conner said. "What matters," he continued, drawing her forward into his arms, "is that you want to be with me."

Mercedes thought her heart would burst. A week ago, she'd never have believed going to the Valentine Ball would make her so happy. But a week ago, she hadn't known Conner.

"You'll go with me?" she asked.

"Of course I will," Conner replied. "I just have to fix it with the Demoses at the Night Owl Club."

"Oh, no! It's a Saturday. I forgot you have to play," she

said in distress. Conner pulled her closer. "It doesn't matter," he said soothingly. "I'm sure they won't care. Most people will be at this Ball anyway, right?" he asked.

"I guess so," she answered.

"Then the Demoses can't complain if I'm there, too. I might even be able to drum up some extra business for the club."

Reassured, Mercedes began to relax. "You're sure they won't mind?" she asked.

"I'm sure," Conner answered. "And I don't care if they do," he said. "On Saturday, February thirteenth," Conner murmured, dropping tiny kisses on her lips, "all I care about is being with you."

"We'll have to go back soon, Mercy," Conner said.

He looked up at the night sky, trying to gauge the time. It was nowhere near dawn, but he should get Mercy back to the Riding Academy soon. Keeping their rendezvous confined to the dead of night was the safest way to avoid interruptions.

Mercedes stiffened a little in his arms.

"I know," she said quietly.

"But not quite yet," Conner murmured, leaning down to kiss her.

There's something wrong, Conner thought. The stiffness of a moment before was still there. He could feel it in her kiss.

"Something's bothering you," Conner said. He took one of the red rose petals and brushed it softly against her cheek. "What is it?" he asked.

Mercedes was silent for a moment. Her face looked strained in the bright moonlight.

121

"Mercy," Conner said again.

"How come you always know what I'm thinking?" she asked with a smile.

"Because I love you," Conner answered. He kissed her again.

"Now," he said. "I want you to tell me what's bothering you."

Mercedes sighed and settled back against him. "I was thinking about Andrea," she said.

Conner felt the night grow cold around him. "Andrea," he said.

"Andrea Burgess, my best friend," Mercedes answered. She fidgeted a little with the sheepskin blanket. "I probably haven't mentioned her."

"You haven't mentioned your *best friend?*" Conner said. Mercedes squirmed uncomfortably.

"We haven't been getting along very well lately," she admitted. There was a tiny silence. "She's been trying to stop me from meeting you."

Conner was quiet for a moment. "Did she try to stop you tonight?" he finally asked. Mercedes looked up at him uncertainly. Then she nodded.

"She came around the side of the stable just as I was leaving with Amber," Mercedes said. "I was being really careful," she said quickly. "But she's been sneaking around after me. There wasn't anything I could do to stop her."

She's still afraid of me, Conner realized, hearing the tension in Mercy's voice. *That's good, my angel of Mercy,* he thought. *That's very, very good.*

"What happened?" he said aloud.

"We had this big fight," she answered. "We're not really friends anymore."

"I don't want to come between you and your friends, Mercy," Conner said. "That's not right."

Mercedes looked up at him anxiously. "You haven't, Conner," she said. "It's all Andy's fault. She's just jealous because I have a boyfriend and she doesn't."

"Well, you have to admit that might be tough on her," Conner said. "She's used to spending a lot of time with you, isn't she?" he asked. Mercy nodded again.

"So, her nose is probably a little out of joint." Conner leaned down and kissed the tip of Mercedes' nose. She smiled up at him.

"Tell me about Andrea," Conner said softly. "What's she like?"

Again, Mercedes squirmed a little. "She comes from this little town in southern Vermont, and she has a big family that's always doing crazy things," she said.

Conner smiled. "It sounds like you know a lot about her," he said. Mercedes nodded.

"I do," she said. "She gets pretty homesick so we spend a lot of time looking at pictures of her family in her scrapbook."

"A scrapbook," Conner said. "She must be very close to her family."

"She is," Mercedes answered. "They're really important to her."

Perfect, Conner thought.

"Would it help it I talked to Andrea?" he said.

Mercedes looked at him, surprise and relief plain in her face.

"It might," she said. "I don't really want to fight with her," she said in a rush. "But I won't let her stop me from seeing you."

And neither will I, Conner thought as he held Mercy tightly in his arms.

"I wish I could see the scrapbook of her family," Conner said carefully. "That way I'd know more about what's really important to Andrea. We'd have something in common. She wouldn't think of me as some stranger who's taking her best friend away from her."

Mercedes shredded a rose petal with great care. "I could bring you the scrapbook," she said finally. "If you really think it would help."

"It would help a lot, Mercy," Conner said. He picked up the pieces of the rose petal and let them fall through his fingers. "It would help me really understand Andrea before I talk to her. But I don't want you to do something you think is wrong," he said.

"No, it'll be all right," she said quickly. Then she reached up and sprinkled a handful of rose petals over Conner's head. "I love you, Conner," she said.

"I love you, too, my angel of Mercy," Conner replied. He rubbed one of the petals back and forth against her mouth.

"Don't worry about Andrea anymore, Mercedes," Conner said, just before he kissed her. "Everything will be all right. I'll take care of her."

Nineteen

MURDER VICTIM IDENTIFIED.
The headline was the first thing Andrea saw as she entered her journalism class on Friday morning. She tossed her shoulder bag down on her desk, went straight for the Cooper Hollow *Herald,* and began to read:

Dateline: February 12, Cooper Hollow, New York.
Police have identified the young woman killed in the old Cooper Hollow graveyard as Elaine Taylor, of Greenbank, Connecticut. Ms. Taylor died almost immediately from wounds she received during a vicious attack on the afternoon of January 30.

Though a massive investigation is currently underway, Homicide Detective Edward Priestly of the Cooper Hollow Police Department indicates there are still no clues as to the identity of Elaine Taylor's killer. Ms. Taylor's parents have declined to be interviewed. A spokesperson for the family states the parents had no idea their daughter had come to Cooper Hollow. They believed she was on a weekend shopping trip with friends in New York.

Police continue to recommend extreme caution in the area of the Cooper Hollow woods between Thirteen Bends Road and Cross Road. Special curfews and safety procedures are still in place at the prestigious Cooper Riding Academy for Girls, site of the old graveyard where the body was found.

Slowly, Andrea folded up the paper and returned to her desk. They'd identified the girl, but not her killer. He could still be in Cooper Hollow, or he could be hundreds of miles away by now. He could be anyone. Anywhere.

But he wasn't just anyone, Andrea thought. He was someone who'd killed a girl her age. How can there be no clues to his identity? she wondered. How can the police still not know anything about him after nearly two weeks?

Sighing, Andrea put down the paper and opened her shoulder bag. Something about that newspaper article bothered her. Something other than the fact that the police said they had no clues to the identity of the person her classmates now referred to as "The Riding Academy Ripper."

The trouble was, she didn't have the faintest idea what.

Face it, Andy, she thought, taking a stack of papers out of her bag and setting them face up on the desk. *You're just looking for an excuse to make things up with Mercy.*

The two friends had had no contact at all since their argument outside the stable. A fact which made Andrea more and more upset. The old Mercy would have come to apologize by now, she thought. But then the old Mercy never would have argued with her in the first place. Or taken her horse to meet a boyfriend in the middle of the night.

Andrea was trying to console herself as best she could

over the sudden loss of Mercedes's friendship. She had to admit she was partly to blame for trying to force Mercy into giving up Conner.

Determined to start her day off on a cheerful note, Andrea had decided to look through her scrapbook first thing this morning. But when she'd opened the bottom drawer of her dresser, she found that the precious photo album was missing. The loss of the album still puzzled Andrea. It made no sense for someone to take it.

Deciding it would turn up soon enough, Andrea's attention went to the papers on her desk. Thumbing through them, she came to her article on Elysian Fields. She couldn't wait to be rid of the article. Couldn't wait to be rid of the band. Quickly, Andrea scanned the article once more, making a last minute check for any errors or typos. Maybe once Elysian Fields had left the area, things would get back to normal between her and Mercy.

That was when she saw it.

Elysian Fields was popular. So popular Andrea had put a special sidebar in her article listing the band's other stops in the New England area. The list had been right there in the press packet Jenny Demos had given her. All Andrea had done was to transpose the names of the tour into her article.

The place Elysian Fields had played just before coming to Cooper Hollow was Greenbank, Connecticut.

For a moment, Andrea thought she was seeing things. *Maybe I got it wrong,* she thought. She scrambled through the press kit, finally finding the page that listed the band's New England stops.

But she hadn't made a mistake. Until the weekend of January 23, Elysian Fields had been in Greenbank, Connecticut. The date of their first performance in Cooper

Hollow was Friday, January 29. The day before Mercedes had discovered Elaine Taylor in the old graveyard.

Andrea set the papers down on her desk. She clasped her hands tightly together to keep them from shaking. *Think,* she told herself, desperately. *Think.*

Okay, she thought. *Maybe it's a coincidence. Now think like a journalist, Burgess. How many other "coincidences" can you uncover?*

Slowly, she went back through the Elysian Fields press kit. She read press clippings and band member bios. *Nothing,* she told herself. *There's nothing here.* The guys from Elysian Fields came from all over the country. They had different backgrounds and interests. There was nothing to link them to the death of a girl in Cooper Hollow, except the fact that the last place they'd played was where the dead girl had lived.

It had to be just a coincidence. After all, it didn't seem very likely that Elaine Taylor would follow a rock and roll band all the way from Connecticut to New York.

And how likely was it that Mercedes Amberson would flip so completely over some guy that she'd do anything he asked, including sneaking off to meet him in the middle of the night with a killer on the loose in the neighborhood?

But she hadn't flipped over "some guy," Andrea thought. She'd flipped over Elysian Fields's lead singer, Conner Egan. Who'd just been in Greenbank, Connecticut.

Andrea closed her eyes and tried to picture Conner Egan. What was it that drew Mercy to him? Had it drawn Elaine Taylor, too? In her mind's eye, Andrea could see Conner's jade green eyes, clear-cut features, and pale blond hair. She remembered the way his hair had blazed under the hot lights at the Night Owl Club. The way the light had reflected off the scarlet ribbon holding it in place.

Andrea felt her stomach begin to tingle. She opened her eyes and stared straight ahead, her eyes unseeing.

What was it Mercy had said to Detective Priestly? The clue he'd thought would lead him to the killer until he'd decided Mercy was simply hysterical? The thing he'd come back to question Mercy about day after day?

"The snow was the color of his hair," Mercedes had said.

The same color as Conner Egan's.

Twenty

"I suppose you think I'm crazy," Andrea said.

She stared down into the cup of tea Jenny Demos had given her after her walk to the Night Owl Club. Getting away from the Riding Academy in the middle of the day hadn't been easy. But the extra riding session Andrea was supposed to put in helped give her a break in the afternoon. Skipping out on her last chance to practice before tomorrow's horse show was something Andy knew she shouldn't even consider. But she couldn't bear another minute of not confiding her suspicions about Conner Egan to someone. Sitting through her morning classes had been agony.

Andrea still wasn't quite sure what had made her come to the Night Owl Club. Maybe it had been the fact that, as she sat through her long morning, the only person she could imagine confiding her troubles in was the young woman who'd seemed so concerned about Mercy the night she'd first met Conner. Jenny had taken Andy's concerns seriously that night. Maybe she would again.

Jenny Demos hadn't seemed at all surprised to discover Andrea pounding on the door of the Night Owl Club in the middle of the afternoon. Though the club was closed,

she'd let Andrea in without a word and fixed a cup of tea to warm her up. Now, the two of them sat in one of the booths around the dance floor. Jake Demos was nowhere to be seen.

Jenny Demos smiled at Andrea's vehement words.

"No, I don't think you're crazy," she said.

Andrea looked up quickly. "But you don't think I'm right, either," she said.

Jenny was silent for a moment, gently swirling the tea leaves in the bottom of her cup.

"I don't think you have enough information to know if you're right or not," she finally said.

"But that's why I'm here," Andrea protested. "I thought maybe, since you and your dad hired Elysian Fields, you'd know more about them."

Jenny sighed and shook her head. She continued to stare into her cup, not looking up to meet Andrea's eyes.

"Dad hired the band based on their notices," she said. "He wanted to try an experiment and bring in somebody who wasn't a local band. Elysian Fields had gotten great reviews in all the other towns they'd played. So he hired them.

"I'm sorry," Jenny told Andrea. "But that's about all there is to tell."

Andrea took a long sip of tea to hide her growing disappointment. She'd been so sure Jenny Demos would be able to help her. Would have information that could help her prove her theory about Conner. But so far, all Jenny had done was to ask questions that made Andrea's brilliant idea look like an umbrella with holes in it. And that left Andrea . . . all wet.

"What about the fact that they'd just played in Greenbank?" Andrea finally asked.

Jenny Demos ran her hand across her forehead as if she had a headache.

"I'll admit it's an interesting coincidence," she said. "Do you think it's one the police haven't discovered?"

She's doing it again, Andrea thought. She was silent for a moment, thinking hard. Elysian Fields had been in Cooper Hollow for two weeks, with the murder investigation going on the whole time. The Cooper Hollow police force was small, but one of the first things they'd do would be to check out anyone who was new to the area. That was standard police procedure. Chances were good the police already knew about Elysian Fields and Greenbank, Connecticut. And they hadn't done anything about Conner Egan, in spite of his pale blond hair.

All of a sudden, Andrea felt completely worn out. She'd been running on nerves ever since she'd decided there might be a connection between Conner and the dead girl. Now, she was beginning to admit that she might have jumped the gun.

"Okay," she said wearily. "I give up."

Jenny Demos reached across the table to clasp one of Andrea's hands in hers.

"Don't give up, Andy," she said. Her voice was low but it vibrated with passion.

"I'm just so worried about Mercy," Andrea burst out, finally confiding the real source of her concern. "She's an entirely different person since she met Conner Egan. It's like she's obsessed. She doesn't care about anything but him."

"Love can be a very powerful force, Andy," Jenny Demos said. "Or maybe I should say, the desire for love. You've always felt loved, haven't you?"

Andrea nodded.

"Do you think Mercy has?" Jenny asked. Andrea knew the answer to that one immediately.

"Not at all," she answered. "She thinks her parents don't care about her and, from what she's told me, I think she's right. The only person who ever really loved Mercy was her grandmother, and she's dead."

"*You* care about Mercy," Jenny said. "Or you wouldn't be here."

"Yes, I do," Andrea answered. She took a deep breath. "And I *don't* think Conner Egan does. He's asking her to do dangerous things. Things that could get her into a lot of trouble. He can't really care about her if he's asking her to do things like that."

"But Mercy doesn't see it that way," Jenny Demos said. Andrea gave her a weak smile.

"You've just made the understatement of the century," she said.

Jenny was silent for a moment. "You're afraid for her, aren't you?" she finally asked.

"Yes, I am," Andy answered quietly.

"What are you afraid of?" Jenny asked.

"I'm afraid he killed that girl in the graveyard." The words burst out of Andrea before she could stop them. "What if that girl felt the same way about Conner as Mercy does? What if she followed him up here, and then he decided she was in the way, and he killed her."

"Do you want to go to the police?" Jenny asked.

It took Andrea a long time to answer.

"No," she finally said. "All I really have is a circumstantial connection between Elysian Fields and the town where the dead girl lived, a connection the police have probably already discovered. The only person who provided any information about there being somebody in the

133

woods with Elaine Taylor was Mercy. And even *I* think she was too upset to really know what she saw.

"Even if the *police* believed me," Andrea continued, "what's Mercy doing hanging out with the guy who matches her own description of the guy in the woods the night of the murder? Mercy can't think Conner is the killer or she'd never go out with him."

Andrea put her head down on her hands. "The police would think I'm crazy, too," she said.

"I don't think you're crazy," Jenny Demos said again. "But I do think you ought to have a long talk with your friend."

"I've tried that," Andrea said miserably. "She won't listen to me."

"Try again, Andrea," Jenny said, her voice deadly serious. "If Mercy is involved in a bad relationship, she needs you more than ever. Don't abandon her just because she won't admit she's in trouble. If she loses you, she won't have anywhere to go when things come crashing down on her. And, believe me, they will."

Andrea lifted her head. For a long moment, she looked into Jenny's strange violet eyes.

"Okay," she said. "I won't give up. I'll try again."

Jenny smiled. "Good," she said.

Andrea slid out of the booth. "I'd better get back," she said. "I'm going to be in big trouble if anyone finds out I've left the Riding Academy." She stood for a moment, awkwardly fumbling with the buttons on her coat.

"Thanks, Jenny," she finally said.

Jenny Demos didn't respond. She continued to sit in the booth, her hands clasped tightly around the tea cup. There was something about her attitude that puzzled Andrea. It was almost as if Jenny was holding something back. As if

134

there was some sort of struggle going on just beneath her friendly surface.

It wasn't until Andrea was almost to the door that Jenny spoke up.

"Andy," Jenny called. Andrea paused to look back.

"Have you thought any more about doing that article on the Night Owl Club?" The sudden change in subject took Andrea by surprise.

"I'd kind of forgotten about it," Andrea blurted. After what they'd just been talking about, how could Jenny care about whether or not Andy did an article on the Night Owl Club?

"Wait a minute," Jenny said. She stood up abruptly and vanished into one of the back rooms of the club. A moment later, she returned with an old leather book in her hand. Again, her strange violet eyes held Andrea's.

"I think you'll find this helpful," Jenny Demos said.

Awkwardly, Andrea took the book and stuffed it into her shoulder bag. She could think about the Night Owl Club later.

"Thanks, Jenny," she said. "I mean, thanks for everything."

"You're welcome Andrea," Jenny said.

She followed Andrea to the door and held it open for her. Andrea could feel Jenny watching her as she crossed the clearing and started back down the path that would take her to the Riding Academy.

It was weird, but just as Andrea turned the bend that took her out of sight, she swore she heard Jenny Demos whisper, "Good luck."

Twenty-one

The pictures were beautiful, even though the people who smiled out at him were ordinary. There was nothing special about them—except the look on their faces that said that nothing could shake their happiness. That they were secure in their love for each other.

Conner Egan hated them. Every single one of them.

He stood in the middle of the path leading from the Riding Academy to the Night Owl Club, slowly turning the pages of Andrea's photo album. It didn't matter that it was too dark to see the pictures clearly. The contents of the album had been burned indelibly into whatever was left of Conner Egan's heart.

He'd sat up all night looking at the photo album. The pictures filled him with rage and longing. This was a kind of love he'd never known. A loved based on a lifetime of understanding, honesty, and trust.

As he'd leafed through the thick, glossy pages, Conner knew again how far from real love what he had felt for Julia McKenzie was. He didn't need any reminders of what *her* feelings had been. His daily existence was reminder enough.

Abruptly, Conner raised his head, listening. *She's coming,* he thought.

Slowly and deliberately, he sauntered over to the side of the path. Why let her know ahead of time that he was here? Much better to surprise her, give her no chance to escape.

Because you won't escape me, Andrea Burgess, Conner thought as he entered the shadows of the trees. *And, if you try to interfere with my plans for Mercy, neither will your lovely, loving family.*

It was colder in the woods than Andrea remembered. The kind of cold that sank into her bones and made her teeth ache. She could hardly wait to be back at the Riding Academy, even if she got into trouble. Her trip to the Night Owl Club had given her a chance to sound out her ideas. But it hadn't made her feel much better. If anything, she was feeling even more confused and worried than before she'd talked to Jenny Demos.

Is there something the matter with me? Andrea thought, as she hurried along the path. Had her concern for Mercy turned her dislike of Conner Egan into her own strange obsession?

Hugging her arms to her chest to keep warm, Andrea hurried through the woods. It was later than she thought, the sun already dipping below the horizon. The lower the sun got, the colder Andrea got. And the colder she got, the more her gut told her that she was right to be afraid of Conner Egan.

Why, Andrea thought to herself. Why would Mercy spend time with somebody who was so bad for her? Why would she be willing to risk being expelled from school

137

and sent back to her unloving parents? Getting *away* from her parents was the reason she'd come to Cooper Hollow in the first place. Her behavior just didn't make any sense.

Unless Conner Egan had some kind of hold on her.

Andrea stopped in the middle of the path, her heart pumping wildly. Why hadn't she thought of that before? she wondered. It would explain Mercy's hysterical insistence that she meet Conner no matter what the cost. What if he had something Mercy needed, something she was desperate for regardless of the consequences?

This is ridiculous, Andrea thought, as she slowly began to resume her walk. The faster her mind raced, the more hopeless the situation looked. What would be powerful enough to make Mercy change her character? And what could have worked so quickly? Mercy literally had been transformed overnight.

Abruptly, Andrea realized her head hurt. It felt as if she'd been clenching her teeth for hours against the cold. *I wonder if you can take two aspirin with a mouthful of snow,* she thought. And then she knew.

Drugs, Andrea thought. That's what he's doing. He's giving her drugs.

She knew there were drugs so powerful it took only one hit to get you hooked. Designer drugs so new they didn't even have names yet. Andrea wasn't quite so naive as to believe that every guy who played in a rock band was a druggie. But she wasn't stupid enough to believe they were all innocent, either.

Now maybe she really did have something she could take to the police. It was true she couldn't *prove* anything, but maybe she could get them to investigate. Even if they only questioned Conner, it might help Mercy.

And if the police can't do anything? Andrea thought.

Then she knew she wouldn't have a choice. She'd have to go to Ms. Chalmers at the Riding Academy. A decision which would almost certainly result in the very thing Andrea had been trying to avoid. Mercy would be expelled.

Andrea tried to picture life at the Riding Academy without Mercy. She didn't think she'd like it much. But, if Conner Egan really was giving Mercy drugs, then she needed help. In a few weeks. Elysian Fields would be gone and Mercy would be left alone. What would happen to her then? The cruelty of it made Andrea furious.

I'll get you, Conner Egan, she thought. *I'll make you sorry you ever came to Cooper Hollow. Sorry you ever hurt my friend.*

And then she screamed.

From out of nowhere, a figure appeared before her on the path, completely blocking her way. Its long, black body seemed to tower over her. Andrea longed to run, but her legs refused to move. She stood rooted to the spot, and watched as the figure reached up with long, pale fingers to push back the hood that covered its face.

"Hello, Andrea," Conner Egan said. "I'm sorry. Did I frighten you?"

For a moment, Andrea was afraid she'd vomit all over Conner Egan's shoes.

Where had he come from? she thought, as she struggled to catch her breath. She could feel Conner watching her. Knew he sensed her battling for control. It suddenly occurred to Andrea that she'd never been this close to Conner before. Never actually had a conversation with him. Up close, it was easy to understand Mercy's attraction to Conner. He really was incredibly good looking.

"Looks can be deceiving." From out of nowhere Jenny

Demos' words popped into her mind. And suddenly, every-thing was very clear.

I don't care what anybody else thinks, Andrea thought. *I know you are evil. I don't know* how *I know it, but I know.* The realization was terrifying. But, somehow, it made her feel better.

"Of course you scared me," she snapped. "You'd scare anybody leaping out of the trees like that. Halloween is in October, you know. If this is your idea of a joke, it isn't very funny." She tried to brush past him. Conner Egan moved to block her way.

"This isn't a joke, Andrea Burgess," he said.

"How do you know who I am?" Andrea snapped again. Stay angry, she told herself. Stay on the offensive. Her anger would keep her strong.

"I've never met you," she said.

"But you know who I am, don't you?" Conner asked.

Andrea backed off a little. "Sure," she answered. "You're Conner Egan, the lead singer for Elysian Fields. I wrote a piece about you for the Riding Academy news-paper."

Conner Egan's eyes narrowed.

"About me?" he asked softly.

"About the band," Andrea answered. *Stupid,* her tone of voice said.

"You don't like me very much, do you Andrea?" Conner Egan said. "Why is that, I wonder?" The chill of Conner's voice went all the way into Andrea's bones.

I must be crazy, she thought. *Even if he's not a murderer, he's dangerous. And I'm standing here arguing with him.*

"I don't really know you," she replied carefully. Conner smiled. Andrea thought she had never seen anything so unfriendly in her life.

"Look," Andrea said. "I'm sorry if I was rude. But you frightened me, jumping out from behind the trees like that.

"Now, if you don't mind, I'd like to get by," Andrea continued. "It's late, and I need to get back to the Riding Academy."

"But I do mind, Andrea," Conner said. Again, he moved to block her way. "There are some things we need to discuss. And I don't think I can let you leave until we do."

"I don't know what you're talking about," Andrea said. Fear began to take hold in the pit of her stomach. "I don't have anything to discuss with you."

"Oh, I think you do," Conner replied. "I think you'd like to talk to me about your friend, Mercy Amberson."

Abruptly, Andrea lost her temper.

"All right," she said. "Let's talk about Mercy. Let's talk about the way she's trailing after you like a dog who's lost a bone. Let's talk about what you're doing to keep her hooked on you."

"You think you've figured that out," Conner said.

"Yes, I think I've figured it out," Andrea snapped. "You're drugging her, aren't you?" Conner Egan made no reply.

"Mercy's not stupid, you know," Andrea continued. "She's smart enough to spot trouble coming when she sees it. The only way she'd hang out with someone like you is if you'd done something to confuse her. Something that made it impossible for her to see what a jerk you really are."

"And that means drugs," Conner said.

"I think it does," Andrea answered. "It's the only thing that makes any sense. But don't think you're going to get away with it."

"You're going to stop me?"

141

"Yes, I'm going to stop you," Andrea screamed. Conner's complacency in the face of her accusations was making her lose control. He just stood there, smiling at her. Her words were hot air. They didn't affect him at all.

"I'll do whatever it takes to stop you," Andrea said.

"Andrea, Andrea," Conner said with a sigh. His voice was filled with sadness and regret. "This isn't going at all the way I'd hoped. I wanted us to be friends. That's what Mercy wants, you know. Mercy wants us to be friends."

"Mercy doesn't know what she wants," Andrea replied.

"What's happened to your friendship, Andrea?" Conner asked, as if he hadn't heard her. "Don't you care about Mercy anymore? Don't you want her to be happy?"

"Happy," Andrea repeated. "Of course I want Mercy to be happy."

Something strange was happening to her. Conner's voice seemed to be all around her. It filled her head and numbed her brain. The voice sounded so sad. So full of concern. Conner was so sorry that Andrea had such terrible suspicions of him. Suspicions that had come between Andrea and her friend. Surely Andrea ought to help him by doing everything she could to make things right. To make things up to Mercy. Wouldn't that be best? That way, Mercy would still be Andrea's friend. They could all be good friends.

What's happening to me? Andrea wondered, with the small part of her mind that still functioned. She could feel Conner's voice moving inside her head. Seeking out the parts of her mind that didn't yet belong to him. When he found them, Andrea knew she would never disagree with Conner Egan again.

I wonder if this is how a mouse feels just before the snake strikes? Andrea thought. Paralyzed and fascinated all at the same time. She remembered reading about how

142

a snake can hypnotize its prey. And she remembered how her brother Bill had put a snake in her bed to see if it would hypnotize her.

At the thought of Bill, the sound of Conner's voice faded a little. Andrea's own thoughts grew clearer and less confused. Desperately, she clung to the image of her brother.

Think about your family, she told herself. *Remember the best things about them. The things that make you laugh. Remember how much you love them.*

And suddenly, Conner's voice was gone from her mind. He was still speaking, but his voice no longer invaded her thoughts. No longer controlled her. He sounded just like any other smooth talker trying to pull a fast one.

"You can save your breath, Conner Egan," Andrea panted. "Other people may fall for your lines, but I won't."

Conner stopped speaking. He stared down at Andrea, his strange green eyes blazing in the growing darkness. He didn't look quite so handsome anymore.

"Andrea Burgess," Conner said. His voice was even colder than the air around them. "You are a surprise. Not many people can resist the sound of my voice. I wonder how much longer you'll be glad you can?

"I think it's time we played a little game, Andrea," Conner said. "You like games don't you? This one is very old. It's called 'Truth or Consequences.' "

Conner Egan smiled and took a step toward her.

"I tell the truth," he said. "And you pay the consequences."

Twenty-two

"You're really very smart, Andrea," Conner said. "I'm quite impressed. But you're not quite smart enough. The hold I have on Mercy is nothing you can possibly imagine."

"Cut to the chase, Conner," Andrea said. "That way neither of us will have to stand around all night."

"Very nice," Conner replied. He took another step closer to her. "Very brave," he said. "I love it when you talk tough, Andy. It almost convinces me you're not afraid of me. But you are afraid, aren't you?" Conner Egan said. "And if you aren't yet, you will be."

Conner stopped his slow advance and gestured toward a fallen tree lying beside the path.

"Have a seat, Andrea," he said. "I'll tell you a story."

"I'm not interested in your stories," she replied.

Conner Egan looked down at her. His strange green eyes glowed in the darkness. Without warning, the fear began; a horrible churning sensation deep in Andrea's gut.

Against her will, she found herself moving. Limbs dragged by some invisible force across the snow. This was even worse than feeling like Conner was trying to get in-

side her mind. This left her mind clear. Clear to watch herself as she staggered to the tree, moving in jerks like some malformed puppet on a string. Clear to know she was absolutely powerless against him.

"I asked you to have a seat, Andrea," Conner said.

Andrea sat down hard, slamming against the fallen tree. And the power released her.

"Now," Conner said. "That's better isn't it?"

Her breath came in ragged gasps. She could taste bile in the back of her throat.

"What are you?" she panted out. Conner gave her a truly beautiful smile. Andrea thought her blood would turn to ice.

"I knew you wanted to know," he said triumphantly. "What I am," Conner Egan told her, "is a vampire."

Andrea was seized by a horrible impulse to laugh.

"A vampire," she said.

"That's right," Conner answered.

"The kind with fangs who go around biting unsuspecting maidens in the middle of the night."

"That's right," Conner Egan said again. "You catch on amazingly fast, Andrea," he continued. "I was afraid I'd have trouble getting you to believe me."

"Believe you," Andrea repeated. She wasn't sure which was worse. Conner as a drug pusher or Conner as a psychopath. Either way, she was in big trouble.

You killed that girl in the graveyard, Conner Egan, Andy thought. *I know you did.*

"You're awfully quiet, Andrea," Conner said. He moved a little closer.

"I can see that you're afraid now. I told you that you would be. I'm glad you're afraid. But I still don't think it's

145

for the right reason. You *don't* believe me, do you? You don't believe that I'm a vampire."

Oh, God, Andrea thought. *I've got to get out of here.*

She looked down at her legs resting against the fallen tree. The legs that had carried her there against her will. And she knew she was never going to make it.

"You're crazy," she said.

"I think," Conner said with another of his beautiful smiles. "That what we need is another little demonstration." He looked down at her. Again, Andrea felt the force of his strange green eyes.

Look away, her mind said. *Look at anything but him.* But it was too late. Her entire body felt like lead. She knew she was never going to move again. Conner Egan was moving slowly and carefully toward her.

His lips were a vivid red against his pale white face. He parted them in a terrible smile and ran his tongue along the edges of his beautiful white teeth. They looked sharp and dangerous. He sat down on the log next to Andrea and pulled her into his lap.

Andrea's body had stopped functioning. But her mind was clear. And filled with a terror unlike anything she'd ever known. She could feel Conner carefully unbuttoning her jacket, loosening the scarf she wore around her neck. She could feel his fingers gently massaging her throat.

"I want you to feel this, Andrea," she heard him whisper. His breath was hot and rank against her neck.

"I want you to know what I'm doing. I could take away your pain and your fear, but I won't. It's time for you to pay the consequences of interfering with me."

She felt his mouth against her neck. His tongue moistening the place between his lips. And then, two sharp

146

pinpoints of pain as he bared his teeth and sank them into her.

His teeth burned as they pierced her flesh. An icy hot that left her howling in agony. She could feel her body buck and thrash. She could hear him swallow as her blood began to run down his throat. With each horrible convulsion, the grip of Conner's teeth grew tighter.

I'm going to die here, Andrea thought. She felt her blood move through her. Rising up out of her body and flowing into his. Soon, the sound of her own heart pounding in her ears was the only thing she could hear.

And then it was over. Andrea gasped for breath, sucking huge gulps of air into desperate lungs. She rolled away from him, falling into the snow. Where she lay, the snow was stained bright red with blood. Her blood. The little blood Conner Egan had left her.

For a moment there was silence. Neither of them moved. Then Andrea felt rough hands on the back of her coat as Conner hauled her back toward the fallen tree. He propped her upright against it. Then he took Andrea by the hair and pulled her head back until she was looking up at him.

The lower half of his face gleamed with her blood. He opened his mouth, baring the disgusting fangs that had let him drain her. His white teeth were still stained a vivid red.

"What am I, Andrea?" he said. His voice was thick and wet. Like nothing Andrea had ever heard before. Like nothing she hoped she'd ever hear again.

"What am I?"

"A vampire," Andrea answered.

And then she fainted.

Twenty-three

Andrea came quietly awake.

Why is it so cold? she wondered. She reached down to pull the bedclothes up a little higher. And her hand encountered a human face.

Screaming, she sat bolt upright, tumbling off the fallen log. Above her, she could hear the sound of laughter. She wasn't safe in her own bed at the Riding Academy. She was still in the middle of the Cooper Hollow woods. With Conner Egan.

And Conner Egan was a vampire.

Andrea surged forward, trying to get to her feet. But her legs buckled under her, and she fell to her hands and knees. Desperately, she began to crawl through the snow. Anything to get away from the horror that was behind her. Anything to be safe. She'd made it almost to the center of the path when Conner spoke.

"What's the matter, Andy?" Conner said. His voice was thick with sarcasm. "Aren't you feeling well? Maybe you'd like a little help getting up."

Without warning, Andrea jerked to her feet and spun

around to face Conner. He propelled her forward until she stood before him.

"This is much easier for both of us, don't you think?" Conner Egan asked. Slowly, he forced her down until she was kneeling at his feet in the snow.

"Now that I've taken your blood, it will be much easier to control you, Andrea," Conner said. "I don't think you'll be doing much interfering from now on."

He sat, relaxed and confident, on the log at the edge of the path. In his hands, he held a white, oversized book. He turned the pages languidly, as if he was reading the paper on a Sunday afternoon.

Andrea made a strangled sound deep in her throat. He had her scrapbook.

"Ah," Conner said with satisfaction. "I see you recognize my reading material. It was nice of Mercy to provide me with it, don't you think? It gave me the chance to learn so much more about you."

He leaned down and grasped Andrea's face. He squeezed until she thought her jaw would snap.

"Listen to me, Andrea Burgess," Conner Egan said. "Mercy Amberson is mine. I've waited two hundred years for her, and nothing is going to interfere with my plans.

"I don't have time to kill you now," he continued. "And your disappearance would just create complications. But make no mistake. I will kill you if I have to. Either way, Mercy will be mine."

He released her, and Andrea felt the blood rush back to where his grip had cut off her circulation. She was sure that every single one of his fingers had left its mark on her face.

"I won't let you," she croaked. It hurt to talk. Like she

was scraping the inside of her throat across ground glass. "I won't let you kill Mercy."

Conner Egan laughed.

"Oh, no, my dear, you misunderstand," he answered. "I have no intention of killing Mercy. Mercy is going to live. She's going to live a long and eventful life. Though not a very happy one. She's going to be a vampire."

Andrea began to wretch, spitting bright blood onto the snow. Conner Egan simply watched. Exhausted, Andrea lay down in the snow and looked up at him.

"Long ago, I loved someone," Conner said. "I swore I would love her forever. I swore I would do anything for her. I killed a man to prove it."

He stopped speaking. For the first time, Andrea thought she saw real emotion in Conner's face. Real suffering and pain. It almost made him look human.

"She made me what I am," he said. "She took my love and turned me into something so horrible I've been running from it for two hundred years."

He smiled, as if enjoying a sad private joke. "Do you know the real reason vampires don't show up in mirrors, Andrea?" he asked. "It's because we can't bear to face ourselves.

"And now Mercy loves me," Conner continued. "She loves me enough to swear to love me forever; to swear she'll do anything to prove her love. And the moment she does that, she belongs to me. I'll drink her hot, sweet blood until there's nothing left in her body. And then I'll be free to live out a mortal life filled with more power than you can possibly imagine."

Conner reached down and gently lifted Andrea from the snow. She had no strength left at all. Conner cradled her in his arms like she was a small child.

"Tomorrow is the day, Andrea," he said softly. "February thirteenth. The eve of Saint Valentine's Day. I like the poetic justice of that, don't you?"

He brushed the snow from Andrea's face.

"I've waited two hundred years to be free, Andrea. Two hundred years to find a victim to greet the dawn of February fourteenth the same way I did. By feeling their love betrayed and their blood slowly draining out of them."

"Nothing is going to stop me from taking my freedom," Conner Egan said vehemently. "Nothing. And if you try, I'll kill you. But first, I'll kill your loving family. Very slowly and very painfully. One by one."

"No," Andrea whispered as she stared up at him. She didn't even have the strength to struggle in his arms. "No."

"Yes, Andrea," Conner said. "Whether I'm a vampire or a mortal, I'll kill them if you interfere with me. So you just think about what's most important to you: Your love for your family or your friendship with Mercy."

Conner stood up abruptly and set Andrea on her feet. He looked down at her, his green eyes holding hers in the darkness.

"Go back to the Riding Academy now, Andrea," he told her. He stepped back and she discovered she could stand.

"Go back and get a good night's sleep. You have to get ready for that big horse show tomorrow, don't you?"

Andrea's legs moved forward, carrying her along the path. Just before she left the trees and entered the Riding Academy grounds, she heard his voice one last time.

"Pleasant dreams," Conner said.

Twenty-four

Tables of girls talked quietly among themselves throughout the dining room. Though everyone carefully obeyed the rule against loud voices during meals, the air was thick with suppressed excitement.

February thirteenth was finally here. It was the day of the February horse show and the Valentine Ball.

Mercedes had started her day by drawing KP duty. It was her job to take orders and deliver food to the girls at her table. She was making her final run with a fresh pitcher of milk when Helen Bledsoe stopped her. Helen's pale blue eyes were sharp with mischief.

"Hi, Mercy," Helen Bledsoe said as Mercedes came to a halt beside her. "All ready for the Valentine Ball?"

Mercedes felt a quick stab of triumph. Two weeks ago, she would have dreaded this moment. She would have crumbled and slunk away, trying to hide her tears in the face of Helen Bledsoe's maliciousness. Two weeks ago, Mercedes had been nobody. Now she was somebody. She was Conner Egan's girlfriend.

"Shut up, Bledsoe," Patty Harris said from the other end of the table. Mercedes turned to smile at her.

"That's okay, Patty," Mercedes said. "I can take care of myself." She turned back to Helen Bledsoe.

"Yes, I am all ready, Helen," she said sweetly. "Are you?"

Helen snickered. "Change your mind about not going stag?" she asked. She stabbed her spoon into the gelatinous mass of her oatmeal.

I wonder if she wishes that were me? Mercedes thought. She'd never understood why Helen didn't like her; she'd tormented Mercedes from her first day at the Riding Academy.

Helen Bledsoe, Mercedes thought. *You are about to be very sorry you ever messed with me.*

"Who said I was going stag?" she asked.

Helen's spoon stopped in midair. A silence spread around the table. It was so quiet, Mercedes could hear the milk drip off Helen's spoon back into her cereal bowl.

"Just everybody," Helen said. But Mercedes knew the conversation wasn't going quite the way Helen had planned it.

Mercedes reached up slowly and tossed her smoky black hair back from her face. There, plain against the vest of her Riding Academy uniform, was the heart-shaped locket Conner had given her. She ran her fingers down the length of the chain until the golden heart dangled from her fingertips.

"I suggest you have 'everybody' check with me first next time, Helen," Mercedes said sweetly. "I'll be going to the dance with Conner Egan."

Helen's spoon hit the side of her cereal bowl, tipping it over and sending milk and oatmeal cascading onto her skirt. Mercedes moved away as Mrs. Alcott surged forward to see what all the commotion was about.

"I hope we see you there," she called back over her shoulder.

It was going to be a beautiful day.

Andrea Burgess woke up screaming.

She lurched upright in bed, tucking her feet under her and sliding back against her headboard. Arms straight out, elbows locked, she tried to fend off her unseen enemy.

"No," she screamed. She writhed, twisting herself up in the sheets, making movement almost impossible. "Stay away from me. No!"

"Andrea," said a voice. "Andrea, what's happening in there? Are you all right?"

Andrea blinked. She was sitting in her own bed at the Riding Academy, tangled in her own bedclothes. The horrible vision had been nothing more than a dream.

"I'm fine," she called out. "Everything's okay. I was just having a bad dream."

The voice on the other side of the door laughed. "It's a little late to be worried about the horse show."

Andrea laughed, too, even though it made her throat hurt. "Yeah, right," she answered.

"You're sure you're all right?" the voice asked again. Finally, Andrea recognized Vanessa Bennett, her neighbor down the hall. "You want me to wait for you?"

"No, really, I'm fine," Andrea answered. "I'll see you at breakfast."

"Okay," Vanessa said. Andrea could hear Vanessa's footsteps as she moved off down the hall.

Slowly and carefully, Andrea unwrapped herself from her blankets and climbed out of bed. She'd never felt so horrible in her life.

154

Her entire body ached. Her throat was raspy and sore. Her head felt like it was on fire, and her hands and feet were like ice.

Maybe I'm catching the flu, she thought, as she staggered over to her dresser mirror. *Wouldn't that be just what I need?*

The face looking back at her was pale and drawn. There were huge circles under her eyes, and a strange pattern of tiny round bruises along her jaw. Vivid red marks ran up one side of her neck, as if she'd scratched her neck raw during the night.

Abruptly, she doubled over, frantically dashing for the sink on the other side of the room. Her hands fumbled with the faucets, sending a stream of cold water into the wash basin. Without hesitation, she plunged her head under the tap, letting the icy water run over her head. She kept it there until she knew she wouldn't puke.

Slowly, Andrea raised her head and reached for a towel. She dried her face and wrapped the towel around her head. Then she turned, and walked slowly back across the room until she stood again in front of her dresser mirror. She unfastened her nightgown and let it slide to the floor.

And then her courage failed her.

I can't look, she thought. *I don't want to know.* And then her eyes fell on what was sitting on top of her dresser, its white cover spattered with tiny drops of dried blood. Her scrapbook.

Moaning, Andrea looked up. She fastened her eyes on her reflection in the mirror and didn't flinch as she turned her head from side to side. The marks were still there, running red and vivid up one side of her neck. And where the marks began, two round scarlet marks like puncture wounds.

Conner Egan's teeth marks.

It hadn't been a dream. The horrible nightmare that had propelled her from sleep had been real. Conner was a vampire. Mercy was going to be his victim. And there was nothing Andrea could do to stop him.

Abruptly, Andrea turned away from the mirror. She opened her dresser and began to put on her clothes. She dressed slowly and carefully. Underclothes; socks. Instead of a button-down shirt, she put on a soft white turtleneck. Its snowy folds completely covered the angry red marks on her neck. She pulled on her work pants and hiking boots. She ran a comb through her spiky blond hair. Then she sat down on the edge of her bed.

What am I going to do? she thought. *I can't just do nothing. What am I going to do?*

But what could she do? Conner had made it perfectly clear that he would retaliate against any attempt Andrea made to interfere by slaughtering her own family. She knew he meant exactly what he said.

And Mercy?

Again, Andrea raised her eyes and looked at herself in the mirror.

I'm the only person Mercy's got, she told herself. Mercy's family didn't give a damn about her. There was only Andy to care about whether Mercy lived or died. Only Andy to stand between Mercy and the unspeakable evil that was Conner Egan.

She had to make one more effort to get Mercy to see the truth about Conner. To get her to change her mind.

I'm Mercy's family, Andrea thought. *And I'm not giving her up without a fight.*

156

Twenty-five

Andrea found Mercedes standing in the hallway outside the Riding Academy ballroom, putting sand and candles into paper sacks.

"What on earth are you doing?" she asked.

Mercedes looked up in surprise.

"Mrs. Alcott says I'm making luminarias," she answered.

"Oh," Andrea said. "What's that?"

"It's a bag with sand and a candle in it," Mercedes replied. Andrea would have laughed if it hadn't hurt her throat so much.

"At night, you light the candles and the bags kind of glow," Mercedes continued. "They're to decorate the front steps and the porch tonight. I think it'll be kind of pretty."

"Hm," Andrea said.

Andrea had decided to take her conversation with Mercedes nice and easy. If she came on too strong, Mercedes would just freak out and walk away. It drove Andrea crazy to stand in the middle of the hallway talking about Mrs. Alcott's party decorations. But she couldn't start their first conversation in three days by marching up and saying, "Oh, by the way, did you know Conner Egan is a vampire?"

I've got to get her to listen to me, Andrea thought. She could feel the panic burning in her chest. *I've got to!*

"Merce," Andrea said. "Is there somewhere we could go talk for a few minutes? I mean, when you're through."

"Sure," she answered, keeping her eyes firmly glued to her project. "We could go take a walk or something."

"Actually, I'm not feeling very well," Andrea said. "Could we stay indoors? Maybe you could just come up to my room."

"Okay," Mercedes said. Her voice was carefully neutral.

"So, I'll see you in a few minutes?"

"Okay," Mercedes said again.

Andrea wished she could see Mercedes' face. But she was keeping all her attention focused on the luminarias, carefully pouring sand into the bags and nestling the candles down into the sand.

Andrea trudged slowly down the hallway and back up the stairs to her room. All the way, she wondered if there *was* a nice and easy way to break it to someone that her boyfriend was a vampire.

"Come in," Andrea called as Mercedes knocked on her bedroom door.

Mercedes wished she knew what to expect from this meeting with Andrea. She was hoping for the best. Hoping that Conner had convinced Andrea that his relationship with Mercedes was a good thing. That way she and Andrea could be friends again.

Mercedes turned the doorknob and stepped into the room.

Andrea was sitting on her bed, slowly turning the pages of her scrapbook. A tiny shiver went down Mercedes' spine

158

"Mercy, you've *got* to stay here. You've got to listen to me! Look, Mercy!" Andrea let go of Mercedes with one hand. She yanked down the collar of her turtleneck to reveal a series of angry red marks running up the side of her neck.

"He did this to me. *Look.*"

Mercedes stopped struggling.

Andrea let go of her and pulled the turtleneck down with both hands, exposing all of her neck. The red marks were vivid and ugly against Andrea's pale, white skin.

"My God," Mercedes whispered. She stepped back, her eyes fixed on Andrea's face.

"He did this to me, Mercy," Andrea continued. "This is what it looks like when a vampire drains your blood."

"My God," Mercedes said again. "You are sick. You are really incredibly *sick.*"

"No," Andrea moaned. She reached out to grasp Mercedes' arm. "Mercy, no. You've got to believe me!"

Mercedes lashed out, breaking Andrea's grip on her arm and sending her crashing to the floor.

"I *don't* have to believe you," she panted. "You did that to yourself, didn't you? Didn't you?"

When Andrea didn't answer, Mercedes began to prowl around the room, throwing Andrea's possessions to the floor. She swept Andrea's shoulder bag, her pens and papers off the desk with a crash. Then she strode to the dresser and picked up Andrea's few toiletries. She leaned against the dresser and threw them, one by one, at Andrea.

Andrea sat in the middle of the floor, surrounded by her belongings and wept so hard she could barely speak.

"How long did it take you to think up that vampire story, Andrea?" Mercedes asked sarcastically. "About fifteen or

twenty seconds?" She took aim with the hairbrush and threw it. It hit Andrea full in the face.

"And then what did you do?" Mercedes continued. Her anger was hot and strong. She'd never felt so powerful. "Scratch your throat until it bled and then think you could convince me Conner had done it?"

Andrea gulped air. "Mercy, please," she said. "You've got to listen to me. You only have until tonight. He said he'll make you a vampire tonight."

"God, you must think I'm stupid," Mercedes said. "What kind of an idiot would fall for a story like that?" She picked up Andrea's one bottle of perfume, the one she'd given Andrea for her birthday, and hurled it to the floor. The sickly sweet smell filled the room.

Andrea put both hands in the broken glass and crawled toward her friend. She grasped Mercedes around the knees. Tears continued to stream down her face.

"Mercy," she croaked. "He'll kill me if he finds out I'm telling you this. He'll kill my family. I'm risking my life for you," Andrea cried as Mercedes tried to break away. "Why won't you believe me?"

"You're crazy!" Kicking out suddenly, Mercedes knocked Andrea away from her. "And you're disgusting. You look disgusting, and you sound disgusting. Your jealousy is disgusting. You make me sick."

She crossed to the door and jerked it open. Then she turned back to Andrea.

"Listen to me, Andrea," she said. "You start spreading any weird rumors about Conner, and I'll go to Ms. Chalmers. I'll tell her you tried to make yourself sick so you wouldn't have to compete in the horse show. I'll make sure you lose your scholarship and have to go home to that

crummy little town in southern Vermont. Now stay away from me," Mercy warned. "Stay away or you'll be sorry."

Then she walked out and slammed the door behind her.

Twenty-six

Andrea sat in the middle of the floor until the smell of perfume made her sick. Then she stood and opened a window.

She stuck her head out through the opening, inhaling huge gulps of cold, fresh air. She looked out over the Riding Academy grounds. The bright sun reflected off the clean, white snow. The grounds hummed with anticipation and excitement. It looked so normal; in spite of the excitement, so peaceful and serene. Nobody had any idea of the incredible evil that existed so close by.

And nobody, including Andrea, could do anything about it.

Pulling her head back in, Andrea sat down on her bed and began to cry. She didn't want to cry again, but she couldn't seem to help herself.

I've got to pull myself together, she thought, as the tears continued to fall. *I can't just sit here and cry. I've got to do something.*

It was if Conner Egan had drained her willpower when he'd drained her blood. And whatever hope he'd left her, Mercedes had all but finished off.

Mercedes would never see the truth about Conner. An-

164

drea knew that now. She was too far gone, sucked too far into his deadly game to ever make a stand against him.

That leaves only me, Andrea thought. And somehow, tears didn't seem like much of a defense against a vampire.

How do you stop a vampire? Andrea wondered. Still crying, she dragged herself off her bed and began to put her room back into some semblance of order. She started with the perfume bottle, picking up the pieces of glass and throwing them in the wastebasket. Her room would smell like Obsession for days, Andrea thought. She wondered whether or not she'd be around for it to bother her.

She wished she'd paid more attention to all those late night horror movies Bill always made her watch. Her brother would know what to do. He'd just whip out a silver bullet or something.

No, not a silver bullet, Andrea thought. *Those are for werewolves.*

Now Andrea started to pick up pens and pencils and return them to neat piles on her desk. Her shoulder bag had flown open when it hit the floor. Its contents were scattered all the way across the room. She crawled on her hands and knees across the floor, too drained to get up. The last item was all the way across the room under the window: an old leather-bound book, the shiny letters on its cover glinting in the morning sunlight.

Tales of Haunted New England.

That's not even mine, she thought, as she picked it up. Suddenly, she'd had enough.

With a cry of rage, she hurled the book across the room. It flew through the air wide open, its pages fluttering from the force of the throw. The sun blazed across the embossed letters on the cover; they seemed to glow with a life of their own.

The book hit the wall with a slap and landed, spine up, on the floor by Andrea's desk. Heart pounding, she crossed the room and knelt down, slowly turning the book over. The words danced and swam on the page as she stared down at them.

The book had landed open at "The Tale of the Cooper Hollow Vampire."

Andrea hit the floor with a *thunk*, her mouth dry and her heart in her throat.

Where did this come from? Her fingers trembled as she frantically flipped through the pages. She began to read the introduction to the chapter:

> *The small town of Cooper Hollow, New York, has been the scene of a number of unusual occurrences. In particular, the area around the old Owl's Head Inn and Tavern, just outside of town, has been the location of a number of unexplained and unfortunate events.*

What Owl's Head Inn and Tavern? Andrea thought. And then she knew.

"Have you thought any more about doing that article on the Night Owl Club?"

In her mind's eye, Andrea could see herself standing at the door of the Night Owl Club facing Jenny Demos. In Jenny's outstretched hand was an old leather book with gilded writing on the cover.

"I think you'll find this helpful," Jenny Demos had said. Looking all the while at Andrea with her serious violet eyes.

Andrea scrambled to her feet, stuffing the book into her shoulder bag and yanking on her coat. She'd gone to see

Jenny once before because she thought the woman might be able to help. This time she was absolutely sure.

Jenny Demos hadn't given Andrea a book called *Tales of Haunted New England* because she wanted her to read up on the Night Owl Club. She'd given it to her because she knew something about Conner Egan.

If it's the last thing I do, Andrea thought, wishing the words weren't quite so appropriate, *I'm going to find out what.*

Twenty-seven

"You knew," Andrea said.

She prowled around the Night Owl Club, unable to sit still, while Jenny Demos watched her from a nearby table. Andrea knew she sounded angry and accusatory, but she didn't really care. She was going to lose. She knew it. And Mercedes was going to be destroyed.

When Andrea had dashed up to the Night Owl Club, she'd found Jenny standing outside, almost as if she'd been expecting her. Without a word, she'd led the way indoors. The club was closed, but the candles were lit on every table. Their flames flickered in some unseen draft, sending grotesque shadows dancing along the walls.

"You knew," Andrea said again when Jenny Demos didn't answer. She pounded on the nearest table. The candle rocked from side to side.

"You *knew* what Conner Egan was and you didn't tell me."

Andrea surged forward, tugging down the collar of her turtleneck.

"Look at this," she commanded. She thrust her wounded neck in Jenny's face. "Take a good look at what Conner did to me after I left here the other day."

168

Jenny looked at Andrea's neck in painful silence.

"You let me walk right out of here without saying anything," Andrea continued. The longer Jenny was silent, the more Andrea's fury increased. "You let me walk away and didn't warn me. I don't understand how you could *do* a thing like that," she cried. "I thought you were my friend."

"I didn't know he was waiting for you, Andrea," Jenny Demos finally said. "And, even if I had, I couldn't have prevented you from leaving. The situation isn't as easy as you think."

"Easy!" Andy yelled. "Who said I think this is easy?"

She stood in the middle of the dance floor, breathing hard and staring at Jenny Demos. Abruptly, Andrea realized that Jenny looked almost as bad as she did. Her face was pale and her eyes were red and puffy. She looked like she'd been crying for hours.

She knows something all right, Andrea thought. *But what she knows doesn't comfort her.*

Andrea's anger departed and only her fear was left, burning cold in the pit of her stomach. She crossed the room and sat down with Jenny.

"I'm sorry, Jenny," Andrea said. She reached across the table to clasp the young woman's hand. "All you've been doing is trying to help, and all I've been doing is yelling at you."

Jenny gave Andrea's hand a quick, hard squeeze. "It's okay," Jenny said. "I know this whole situation must be difficult for you to understand."

Andrea ran her hands over her face as if to clear her mind. "Okay," she said. "Let's just make sure that we're really talking about the same thing here." She took a deep breath and looked steadily at Jenny Demos.

169

"True or false," Andrea said. "Conner Egan is a vampire."

A faint smile appeared on Jenny's face. But her eyes stayed deadly serious. "True," she said quietly. "Conner Egan is a vampire."

The fear in Andrea's gut made her stomach ache. "True or false," she said again. "He wants my friend Mercy to be one, too. And I'm the only one who can stop him."

Jenny's violet eyes flickered in the candlelight as she looked across the table at Andrea.

"True."

Andrea felt the color drain slowly from her face. Until this moment, she'd been hoping she'd made a mistake. Hoping the cavalry would arrive in time to save her. Now, she knew it was too late. She was the only thing that stood between Mercy and Conner Egan. And she wasn't strong enough to stop him.

She put her head down on her hands. "Can't you help me?" she whispered.

"Yes, I can," Jenny said.

Andrea lifted her head. The pain in her gut began to diminish.

I'm not alone, she thought. *It's going to be okay.*

"And, no, I can't," Jenny continued.

Andrea shook her head. "I don't understand," she said.

"I can advise you," Jenny answered. "I can answer questions; provide information. But I can't fight alongside you. I can't take direct action against him."

Andrea jumped up from the table and began, again, to prowl around the room.

"Why?" she cried. "I don't understand *why.*"

"We don't have time to go into that now, Andrea," Jenny

170

said. "Right now, you need to think of a way to stop Conner Egan."

"How can I think of a way to stop him?" Andrea exploded. "I don't know anything about vampires."

Jenny shook her head. "You never read *Dracula?*" she asked. "You never watched any late night horror movies?"

"No," Andrea said with a sarcastic laugh. "I suppose you think I should have spent my life preparing for my big encounter with a vampire. Well *excuse me.* It never occurred to me I'd be meeting one."

Jenny was silent for a moment.

"Okay," Andrea finally said. "Maybe I watched one or two movies with my brother. But that doesn't mean I know anything that will *help.* All I can remember is something about garlic and silver bullets. No, wait a minute." She sat down on the edge of the band platform. "Not silver bullets. Something else. A wooden stake through the heart."

"That's right," Jenny Demos said. "Garlic won't actually kill a vampire, but it will slow one down. They don't like the smell. And a stake through the heart is usually the most effective way to kill one."

Andrea picked up the strange inflection in Jenny's voice right away.

"Usually?" she asked. Jenny nodded in approval.

"I'm not sure a stake through the heart will work in Conner's case," she said. "He's a little unusual, even for a vampire."

"Oh, that's just great," Andrea said. "It's not hard enough to fight a regular vampire. Mine has to be someone special."

In spite of herself, Jenny smiled.

"Okay," Andrea said. "What's so unusual about Conner?"

171

"Most vampires always have with them some of the earth in which they were buried," Jenny said. "Your brother could probably tell you that lots of horror movies show vampires in their coffins during the day. That's nice and theatrical. But it isn't the coffin that's important. It's the *earth* around it. It's a source of power for them. But it also makes them vulnerable. Because once you've found the earth, you've found the vampire's hiding place."

"But not Conner," Andrea said.

"Conner's never been buried, Andrea," Jenny Demos explained. "He never died and then returned to life the way other vampires do. He literally took the place of the vampire who created him. It was more like an energy transference."

Andrea nodded. "That's what he's going to do to Mercy," she said. "He said he would make her what he is, and that then he'd be free to live out his mortal life." She paused for a moment, searching her memory.

"He said it would be a life of unlimited power," she finally said. "That he could have whatever he wanted for as long as he lived."

"That's right," Jenny Demos answered. "It's not much for the rest of us to look forward to, is it? About the best we can hope for is that he won't want to stay anywhere near Cooper Hollow. There's not much reason to think he'll suddenly turn into Mr. Nice Guy just because he's no longer a vampire."

"My family," Andrea whispered. "He said if I tried to interfere with him, he'd kill my family. Even if he became a mortal."

Jenny was silent for a moment. Then she said, "We could stop this conversation now, Andrea. You haven't actually tried to take any action against Conner. All we've

172

been doing is talking. You can walk away now, and your family may still be safe."

"What about Mercy?" Andrea asked.

Jenny Demos didn't answer.

"She'll never make it, will she?" Andy answered her own question. "Even if he doesn't turn her into a vampire, he'll need her blood to keep on going. And he won't have any reason to let her live. He'll kill her. And I'll spend the rest of my life wondering if I could have saved her."

"You *can* save her," Jenny said.

"For God's sake, how?" Andrea said. "You just got done telling me a stake through the heart isn't going to work. What other choice is there?"

"Use your brain, Andrea," Jenny Demos said angrily. "You've got all the information you need to bring Conner Egan down. But you won't stop whining long enough to figure out what it is."

Andrea stared at Jenny. Jenny always had been quiet and supportive. Andrea had never imagined she could get so angry.

"When have you seen Conner, Andy?" Jenny pressed her. "When does he ask Mercy to meet him?"

"At night," she replied. "At night; at night; at night." She broke off suddenly, breathing hard. "Oh, my God, that's it isn't it? The thing even an *idiot* knows about a vampire. You just said it, and I didn't pay any attention. They only come out at night."

"Why do they only come out at night, Andrea?" Jenny said.

"Because they can't stand the sunlight. Sunlight destroys them. Sunlight."

"Yes," Jenny Demos whispered. "Yes."

"Well, that certainly solves everything," Andrea said. "What am I supposed to do? Push him under a sun lamp?"

She sat back down on the edge of the band platform and put her head in her hands. "Conner's not going to stand around waiting for the sun to come up, Jenny," she said. "He's going to take Mercy somewhere. Wherever it is he goes during the day. That's where he's going to turn her into a vampire."

"I think you're right," Jenny said.

Andrea lifted her head. Across the light of the flickering candles, she stared at Jenny Demos.

"You know where it is, don't you?" Andrea said. "You know where Conner goes during the day."

"Yes," Jenny answered. Her face wavered in the candlelight. And then, incredibly, she began to cry.

Very, very slowly, Andrea got to her feet.

"It's here, isn't it?" she said.

Jenny Demos wiped her face.

"Conner wants the poetic justice of claiming his final victim in the same place where he became a vampire," Jenny said. "He wants to pass the place on as both a source of power and a source of torment. And that place is here, at the Night Owl Club."

Twenty-eight

Mercedes stood in her room, slowly dressing for the February horse show.

It seemed ridiculous to be putting on her riding habit when she wasn't going to compete. But that was the rule. Every Academy girl went in riding attire, even if she wasn't participating. It was a show of school spirit and solidarity.

Mercedes hadn't been looking forward to the horse show very much.She'd always found it depressing to sit in the stands and watch her peers perform elaborate tricks she knew she was never going to perform herself. Before, events like the horse show had only been upsetting to Mercedes. They seemed tailor-made to highlight the fact that she really didn't belong at the Cooper Riding Academy. That she had nothing but wealth in common with most of her classmates.

But Mercedes' encounter with Helen Bledsoe had changed all that.

Mercedes smiled at her reflection in the mirror as she buttoned up her blouse. She took extra care to remove Conner's locket from under the clean, white cloth and place it on top of the shirt, where it would be plainly vis-

ible. She had no doubt that word of her date with Conner had spread through the entire school by now. And that was just fine with her. The more people there were who knew that Mercy Amberson was someone to be reckoned with, the better.

Why did it take me so long to fight back? Mercy wondered. *How could I have been such a wimp?*

It must have something to do with Andrea, she decided, reaching for her bottle of perfume. Andrea had kept Mercy dependent on her. Kept Mercy from asserting herself and assuming her true position in the social life of the school.

Maybe I should have gone to Ms. Chalmers anyway, Mercy thought, as she dabbed a little scent behind her ears. Maybe Andy was dangerous. Maybe she should be locked up or sent away. Somewhere far from Conner and Mercy.

She was so lost in her thoughts she didn't hear the knock on her door.

"Hey, Mercy. Are you in there?" Without waiting for an answer, the speaker turned the doorknob and stuck her head in the door. It was Patty Harris.

Mercedes jumped and banged the perfume bottle back down on the dresser. Patty smiled apologetically.

"I'm sorry," she said. "I didn't mean to scare you. But you didn't answer the door."

"It's okay. You didn't scare me," Mercedes said. She smiled back at Patty. "I guess I didn't hear you knock. What's up?"

"I came to see if you knew where Andy was," said Patty. "She hasn't been in the stable all morning. I wondered if you knew what happened to her."

"Haven't a clue," Mercedes said, turning away from the door.

She shrugged into her riding jacket and rearranged Con-

176

ner's locket to make sure it was still in plain sight. She turned from side to side in front of her mirror, admiring the effect. The locket glowed against the black of her riding jacket. There was no way anyone would miss it.

"Did you try her room?" she asked. In her mind's eye, she could see Andrea sitting in the middle of her bedroom floor and weeping.

Patty Harris nodded.

"She's not there," she answered. "Or if she is, she's not answering the door."

Mercedes could feel Patty Harris watching her. She looked up and met Patty's eyes in the mirror. The other girl's face was puzzled and concerned. Mercedes held her gaze until Patty looked away.

"Well, if you're sure you don't know where she is," Patty said at last.

"I told you," Mercedes said coldly. "I don't have any idea."

"Okay," Patty said, backing out of the door. "See you at the show."

"See you," Mercedes answered. "Good luck."

The door closed with a soft click, leaving Mercedes alone in front of the mirror.

Who cares *about Andrea and the stupid horse show?* Mercy thought. She scooped up her riding hat and set it on her head at a rakish angle. She wished the horse show was already over so she could move on to the most important event of the day—the Valentine Ball.

She took a couple of dreamy dance steps as she made her way to the door. Tonight everybody would know that Mercy Amberson wasn't just another Riding Academy girl.

They'd see for themselves how important she was to Conner Egan.

Twenty-nine

Andrea stood in the quiet of Midnight's stall, leaning with her eyes closed against the huge, dark horse. Spending time with Midnight always comforted her. But Andrea had never dreamed she'd need her horse's comfort quite as much as she did today.

Today should have been a day for Andrea to focus exclusively on the horse show. Instead, even standing in Midnight's stall she was thinking about Mercy. Her fear for Mercy ran through her like hot wire. It made her tense and jumpy. It threatened to block out every other thought.

It had been agony to leave the Night Owl Club knowing Conner Egan might be somewhere near. But time had run out on Andrea Burgess. She couldn't spend the afternoon searching for Conner. She had to return to the Riding Academy to take part in the horse show.

With a sigh, she stepped back from Midnight's warm flank and reached for the brush and currycomb. Horse show judges didn't just pay attention to the rider. They also looked closely at the horse to make sure it was groomed properly and was a good representative of its breed. Mid-

night's appearance and performance were just as important as Andrea's.

She ran the brush and currycomb over Midnight, adding a final lustre to his already gleaming coat. She checked the ribbons braided into his mane and tail to make sure they were still neat and tight. If Andrea was going to compete, she had to do it properly. Her riding skills were part of her ticket to the Riding Academy. She had to perform well at the show if she wanted to stay.

She imagined herself in Ms. Chalmers' office, explaining to the headmistress that she couldn't compete in today's event because she had to save Mercy Amberson from her boyfriend, the vampire. Then she imagined herself being sent home in disgrace. In a straitjacket.

Andrea finished checking Midnight's mane and gave the horse's head a quick pat. She ran her hands along his withers and down his legs, checking for anything unusual. Midnight stamped impatiently. He knew he was fine. And he was ready for action. Andrea gave his rump a swat and turned to look around the stall.

What did the well-equipped vampire fighter take along to get the job done? Andrea wondered. She opened the duffel bag she'd brought down from her room, wishing she had some of Bill's chemicals, the ones that exploded on contact with water. Or better yet, with vampires.

Andrea put in a strong length of rope. Rope always came in handy. She had no idea what sort of device kept the sunlight out of Conner's room, but she was betting on the fact that it was something she could take apart or tear down. She added a leather longe, used in training to guide a horse around a ring. The longe was strong, but it was thinner than the rope. Thoughtfully, she put in a length of stirrup leather with the heavy metal stirrup still attached.

Then she left Midnight's stall and walked to the stable's community tool room.

She rummaged in the tool chest and found a crowbar and a hammer. She took two picket stakes and lashed them together in the shape of a cross. She wasn't sure whether that would do any good. But she'd take it, just in case. She'd hit the kitchens later for some garlic.

Andrea zipped up the duffel bag and checked her watch. It was nearly lunch time. Time to go change and grab a bite to eat before the show. Then she could come back, saddle up Midnight, and put him through the first part of his warm-up.

The horse show officially opened at 3:00 P.M. Already, out-of-town competitors were beginning to arrive. Ms. Chalmers would conduct the opening ceremonies and then the first round of competition would begin.

Andrea snatched up the bag and headed for the stable door. The duffle banged against her shins as she walked. She crossed the grounds and headed for her room, wishing she didn't feel quite so nervous. Her preparations seemed ridiculous and puny. Conner Egan was incredibly powerful. She'd had ample evidence of that. How was she going to stop him with a length of rope and a crowbar?

She took a firmer grip on the duffel and started up the stairs to her room. *I won't give up hope,* she thought fiercely. *I won't.*

Because she *did* have hope. Hope that Conner's power would be his downfall. That he believed he was invincible and would grow careless. In that case, Andrea might just have a fighting chance.

I've done the best I can, Andrea thought. The only thing left was what Jenny had suggested.

She'd have to use her brain. She hoped it was as good as Conner Egan's.

And that her luck was even better.

Thirty

A steady stream of spectators poured into the indoor ring at the Cooper Riding Academy for the February horse show. Although the shows in warmer weather drew bigger crowds, the February horse show was particularly important for the girls of the Cooper Riding Academy. A good showing on their home turf always enhanced the Academy's prestige.

The snow sparked and squeaked underfoot as Mercedes joined the crowd making their way to the big indoor ring. It was an almost perfect day. The sky was cloudless and clear, its color the piercing blue that hinted at the end of winter.

Ms. Chalmers stood in the center of the ring on a podium brought in especially for the occasion. The severe black of her riding habit suited the headmistress' sharp, angular features. Ms. Chalmers was always at her best during a horse show.

Mercy clambered up to the back of one of the bleacher sections and looked out across the ring.

Like the girls of the Cooper Riding Academy, students from other schools had come dressed in riding attire, even

if they weren't competing. The ring was a sea of black jackets, cut occasionally by the bright red of a rider in the Hunter class. The cold afternoon sunlight streamed in through the high arena windows.

Ms. Chalmers stepped up to the podium microphone and cleared her throat. She waited until the ring was almost silent before she began to speak.

"Good afternoon, ladies and gentlemen," Ms. Chalmers said. "It is with a great deal of pleasure that I welcome you all to the Cooper Riding Academy for Girls." The crowd of spectators applauded politely.

"As you know, the February horse show is an annual event here at the Cooper Riding Academy. I hope you will join me in wishing our competitors from around the region the very best of success." Again, the crowd applauded politely.

"And now," Ms. Chalmers said, raising her voice. "It is my pleasure to welcome to this arena the young women who will be competing in this afternoon's events." She lifted her arms as if she were a queen summoning her court to an audience.

"Girls," she said.

And then the riders appeared. They cantered around the ring to the enthusiastic applause of the crowd. Mercedes had no difficulty locating Andrea. The contrast of her pale coloring against the black of her horse made her easy to spot.

The riders completed two circuits of the ring and then came to stand before Ms. Chalmers.

"It is a very great honor to be competing in this arena today," Ms. Chalmers said. "I feel sure that all of you will represent your schools to the best of your abilities. I know you will make us proud."

The riders joined the crowd in a final cheer, then wheeled their horses around and headed for the main exit of the ring. Ms. Chalmers descended from the podium and several stable hands came to carry it away. The judges began to come out into the center of the arena. The crowd shifted restlessly as they waited for the first event to begin.

Mercedes watched as the first group of riders entered the ring.

They moved in single file around the outside of the ring, each horse moving at a carefully controlled walk. Mercedes knew it was important for each rider to demonstrate proper seat position and control of the horse. You couldn't just let your horse follow the one in front of him. You had to show that every move your horse made was at your command. And you had to make it look like you'd never given a command. The team of horse and rider had to behave like one animal.

In the center of the ring, the judges turned and pivoted as they watched individual girls perform. They made notes on clipboards. Then, at the judges' signal, the entire group completed a change of hands and began to trot.

Again, the horses made a circuit of the ring, this time in the opposite direction. Mercedes began to concentrate on the individual performances of the people she knew. Patty Harris always looked great. Her horse was a beautiful bay mare called Clover Honey. Their passes around the ring looked controlled yet effortless. Andrea and Midnight were right behind her.

Now the judges began calling individual riders into the center of the ring. The horses stood stock still as the judges walked around them. Then, at the judges command, the horse and rider executed a series of moves designed to further demonstrate control and flexibility. They turned in

circles. They backed up, making sure the backward walk was as smooth and even as the forward one.

Mercedes began to squirm a little on the hard bleacher seat. Who cares whether a horse can back up or not? she thought. She drew a couple of angry looks from spectators seated near her and sat still.

One by one, the individual riders were called into the center of the ring and put through their paces. Then, the entire group demonstrated the final gait, the canter. They moved quickly and smoothly around the ring until, at the judges' signal, they came to a halt and formed a line across the center of the arena.

The judges took several moments to confer while the riders sat motionless on their horses. The girls from the Cooper Riding Academy were lined up together. Andrea sat quietly between Patty Harris and Andy's floor mate Vanessa Bennett.

Now that Andy was still, Mercy could see plainly how pale and tired she looked. Her face was fixed in a concentrated frown instead of the usual joyful expression she wore while riding. She blinked rapidly, as if clearing sweat from her eyes. Even at distance, it was clear that she wasn't feeling well.

The judges announced their decision, and the crowd responded with enthusiasm as Patty Harris on Clover Honey moved forward. She took one complete circuit of the ring, waving to the applause of the crowd. Then she led the riders out of the arena.

The first round of competition was over.

Thirty-one

Andrea barely made it back to the warm-up ring.

She slid off Midnight's back the moment she entered the covered enclosure, grateful to have her feet on solid ground. Even the simplest part of the competition had taxed her strength, made her head hurt so badly that every movement of her horse had been sheer agony. And the most difficult part of the competition was yet to come—to say nothing of what Andrea would try to accomplish later in the evening.

Andrea knew she was in big trouble.

She walked Midnight slowly around the ring, cooling them both down and trying to focus on the tasks immediately ahead of her. At least she had a break now, Andrea thought. The competition had kicked of with the more advanced riders and would now feature the novice classes in their events. Later, she'd have to return to the ring for advanced dressage and what was usually her best event, the stadium jumps that made up the steeplechase.

She put Midnight on a longe and continued to exercise him. She didn't want to get him all worked up, but neither of them could afford to get too cold between events. As

she moved slowly around the warm-up ring, Andy tried to picture the steeplechase course in her mind. No one knew exactly in what order the jumps would occur, but there'd probably be at least ten different obstacles for her to jump over. Ten opportunities to send Midnight flying through the air. And, the way she was feeling right now, that added up to ten opportunities for complete disaster.

The cold air of the outdoor ring felt good on Andrea's face. The ring was protected by a tent, but the temperature was pretty much the same inside as it was outside.

Andrea pulled deep breaths of cold air into her lungs and began to feel a little better. She wondered suddenly if her illness was part of Conner Egan's plan. Part of the way he'd keep her out of the way and under control. He'd use her own body and her own fear to defeat her.

Andrea felt a quick spurt of anger and pulled another breath of air deep into her lungs. Again, she felt her head clear a little. She began to move faster, urging Midnight into bigger circles at the end of the longe. After a few minutes, she removed the longe and got back onto her horse. She moved steadily around the warm-up ring, concentrating on feeling the rhythm of the powerful animal beneath her. Concentrating on the joy, the incredible feeling of being *alive* riding always gave her.

By the time she finished, the sun was burning low in the late winter sky. Andrea knew that advanced dressage would probably be the last event performed while it was still daylight. The powerful lights in the indoor arena would already be turned on. The final event, the steeplechase, would take place after dark.

"Hey, Burgess," she heard Patty Harris call. "Let's go. It's time for me to pound you into dust in another event."

187

Andrea laughed and brought Midnight around. She brought her horse abreast of Clover Honey.

"Watch yourself, Harris," Andrea said. "The bigger your head gets, the harder it's going to hurt when you fall."

Patty Harris gave her quick and easy laugh. She reached over to grasp Andrea's arm.

"I'm glad you're feeling better," she said. Andrea smiled back at her. Her head felt clear and strong. She wasn't out of any competition yet.

"Me, too," she said.

The two girls left the warm-up ring together.

Thirty-two

Conner Egan came suddenly awake. He opened his eyes to the clear, cool darkness of February 13, his mind burning with a single thought.

After two hundred years of waiting, he would claim his final victim tonight.

He stretched like an alley cat, feeling his long, hard muscles extend and contract. There was no one to stand in the way of his freedom, Conner thought. No one strong enough to prevent him from working his will. He was invincible.

Nothing could stop him from obtaining his desire.

Nothing.

He laughed—a hard, cold sound cutting through the evening air. He lifted his head and sniffed, like a predator scenting the wind. And then the rage that was never far from Conner's handsome surface rose up to overwhelm him.

She had been here. He could feel it.

He had threatened her, threatened her family and still she returned to trouble him. It was true that he didn't know exactly what Andrea had been doing that day at the Night

Owl Club. But the fact that she'd come at all was proof that she needed another lesson in the completeness of his power.

Conner swung his legs over the edge of the four poster bed and sat for a moment, considering.

Perhaps an early visit to the Cooper Riding Academy, Conner thought. A courtesy call at the horse show. If Andrea had an accident there, it would seem entirely her fault. No foul play would be suspected.

Conner smiled. It would be fun to toy with her. Terrorize her until she lost her nerve. Why not, he thought. After all, it was a special occasion. A special night for him. And for Mercy and Andrea. Why not do everything in his power to make sure it was a night neither of them would ever forget?

Conner was still grinning when he left his room and headed purposefully toward the Cooper Riding Academy for Girls.

The hot lights of the indoor ring beat down on the competitors in the steeplechase. Andrea sat on Midnight's back, looking out over the course and trying to still the pounding of her heart. This was going to be harder than she expected.

She'd been right about the total number of jumps, ten in all. But several of them were combinations, requiring the horse to jump, stride, and jump again. Combinations were always tricky. A hesitation or a false step anywhere could make the obstacles hard to clear. And knocking down rails added fault marks to your score. Throughout the course, no two obstacles were exactly alike, presenting both horse and rider with the test of a variety of heights and surfaces.

The final obstacle was a brick wall with a water jump immediately beyond it. Of course the wall wasn't made of real bricks. But, other than that, the Riding Academy had gone all out. The course was a first-class representation of the kinds of jumps you might actually encounter in the field. There was even real water in the water jump. And it looked deep.

Andrea stroked Midnight's neck, hoping the action would calm them both. The horse had caught her nervousness, a bad sign. She *had* to feel confident and communicate that confidence to Midnight if they were going to make a good run.

She watched the first girl take the course. It was someone Andrea had never seen before, someone from an upstate school. She got into trouble almost right away, knocking down the top rail on the third jump. Horse and rider struggled to reestablish their rhythm through the rest of the course. But the horse strained through the combinations and landed in the water at the end of the course. Andrea could tell her first assessment had been correct. The course was a tough one.

Vanessa Bennett went next. Andrea liked Vanessa, who roomed just down the hall from her. She was quiet and serious, and she never seemed to be into the power games that occupied a lot of the other girls. Andrea was pleased to see Vanessa execute an almost flawless run. Her only difficulty came in the second combination, a difficult three jump sequence called the Devil's Dike. Andrea tried to feel the rhythm of the jumps as Vanessa went through them.

Jump, one stride. Jump, two strides. Jump. If she could internalize the rhythm, she stood a better chance of communicating it to Midnight.

Vanessa finished her run and cantered back to the en-

trance of the ring. She made a face at Andrea, who grinned in return. She and Midnight were up next. Andrea moved Midnight into the starting position and waited for the signal from the judges.

Andrea and Midnight cleared the low brush jump with ease. Immediately, they turned sharply, proceeding in a diagonal across the inside of the ring and working up enough momentum to take a railroad gate and the first combination. The railroad gate went flying by and then Midnight was sailing over the parallel rails that had been the downfall of the first competitor. With only one stride in between, he cleared the stone wall that was the second part of the combination. Then they were into the long, slow turn that prepared them for the diagonal that would take them back across the ring. So far, everything was going perfectly.

They were half way into the turn and heading for the gate jump when Andrea began to feel the pulsing in her neck. A steady, painful throb in exactly the same rhythm as Conner's swallows as he'd drained her blood.

Midnight cleared the gate jump and completed the turn. Now they were headed straight for the Devil's Dike.

That was when she saw him. Silhouetted against the dark, open door of the riding arena. His pale blond hair was pulled back, but his face was still in shadow. All Andrea could see clearly were his dark red lips as he ran his tongue across them and then parted them slowly in an obscene smile. And the cold fire of his strange green eyes.

It was Conner Egan.

Midnight snorted and rolled his eyes. Andrea wasn't sure if he could see Conner, or if the horse was reacting to her fear. An entire section of the audience faced the

door where Conner was standing. But she was the only one who seemed to see him.

It's in my mind, Andy thought. *He's not really there. It's all in my mind. He just wants to torment me.* The pulsing in her throat increased.

Now they were into the Devil's Dike, and Andrea began to feel like she was riding through an inferno. Jump, one stride. Jump, two strides. Jump. Andrea never knew how Midnight made it. Huge, shimmering heat waves rose up from the floor. The air was so stifling she thought it would choke her.

Midnight picked up speed as they prepared for the circle that would take them through the jumps around the outside of the ring and set them up for the final obstacle. Andrea watched in horror as the big horse moved forward. Now they were headed directly for Conner Egan.

Midnight wheeled into the first turn and Conner vanished, disappearing before Andrea's eyes like smoke in the wind. Abruptly, the pain in her neck increased. Now it was so intense, Andrea fought to stop herself from dropping the reins and clawing at her shirt.

Please, Andy thought. *Please let this be over.* She no longer concentrated on anything but getting through the course. Getting through the pain. She felt as if she'd been in the arena for hours.

Together, she and Midnight flew down the outside of the ring. One jump, then two were over. They completed yet another turn at the far end of the track and went back through the third combination. Jump, one stride. Jump. Then they were over the final obstacle before the sweep to the brick wall and the water jump.

The pain in Andrea's throat began to ease a little. They were almost through. Midnight was doing everything in

his power to demonstrate his support for his rider. Andrea knew their flawless run was due almost entirely to the efforts of the horse.

They entered the final curve and headed straight for the brick wall. Andrea could feel the strength in Midnight's hind legs as he gathered himself for the long final jump.

And then she screamed and pulled back on the reins, sending Midnight crashing down into the obstacle. From out of nowhere, Conner Egan had materialized in front of her, floating in the air directly in her path, his arms reaching out as if he would embrace her.

Andrea flew forward, tumbling over Midnight's head, and plunging downward, into the water behind the brick wall.

As the icy water closed over her head, Andrea could see Conner's fingers reaching down to hold her there forever.

Thirty-three

His arms were tight around her. They held her in place or moved her where he wanted her. She felt like a rag doll, limp and fluid in his arms. Her body and soul were in his power.

It was the most wonderful feeling in the world.

Mercedes Amberson lifted her head from his chest and smiled up at Conner Egan.

The Valentine Ball was in full swing. For hours students from the Cooper Riding Academy, and their dates and guests had been rocking to the tunes of Talking Ravens, one of the hottest local bands. They couldn't compare to Elysian Fields, of course. Everyone agreed on that.

Conner's appearing with Mercedes had created quite a stir. They made a stunning couple, Mercedes' dark hair and eyes were the perfect complement to Conner's pale good looks. She was dressed in flowing white, her hair caught back from her face by a circlet of tiny, blood red roses. A long stemmed rose of the same color stood out vividly on the front of her dress. The beautiful golden locket shone against her skin.

The dress was one of Granny Amberson's, a costume

she'd had made for one of the fancy dress balls she'd thrown as a young woman. From the moment Conner had said he'd go to the Valentine Ball with her, Mercy knew it was the dress she would wear. The costume was from the Revolutionary War period.

Conner was a study in light and shadow. His clothing was modern, but something about it seemed to suggest it belonged to the same period as Mercedes'. The tight fit of the black coat accentuated his lean, muscular frame. As he did when playing with Elysian Fields, Conner held his long blond hair back from his angular face with a red silk ribbon.

For hours, Mercedes had enjoyed the envious looks directed her way. It seemed there wasn't a girl in the room who wouldn't be happy to change places with her. Gone was the feeling that Mercedes didn't belong, that she was nobody at the Cooper Riding Academy. Instead, she was riding high with triumph. Conner had chosen her. Placed her above everyone. And she was never, ever going to fall back down again.

She smiled dreamily as he held her in his arms. Conner smiled back at her.

"What are you thinking, my angel of Mercy?" he said. Mercedes blushed and didn't answer. Conner bent his head, his lips brushing her ear.

"Have I told you how beautiful you look tonight?" he murmured. "Have I told you I've never seen anyone look as beautiful as you do?"

Mercedes stood, swaying gently in the circle of his arms, and looked up at him.

"Nobody?" she asked softly. She hoped Conner couldn't hear the tiny catch in her voice.

Conner moved his hand against her back, tangling it in

her long dark hair. He pulled her head back gently until all Mercy could do was stare up at him.

"Nobody, angel of Mercy," Conner said. "You're the one I want. The only one. Now and—"

"Forever, Conner," she said. "I'll love you forever."

Passion blazed across Conner's face. His pale cheeks flushed with sudden color. His eyes glowed like emeralds. Heedless of the crowd of people around them, he bent his head and gave Mercy a long, searing kiss. Mercy felt as if her soul were in her lips.

Everything I have is yours, Conner, she promised silently. *Everything.*

A smattering of applause and laughter broke out as Mercedes and Conner ended their embrace. She blushed and laughed with the couple standing next to them. She didn't recognize the guy. The girl was Helen Bledsoe.

So much for you, Helen Bledsoe, Mercedes thought. *You've seen how much Conner wants me. You've all seen.* She gave Helen a smile full of triumph.

"Come on, Conner," Mercedes said, just loud enough for others around her to hear. "Let's go get some air. It's a little too crowded in here for me."

Again the people around them tittered with laughter. Everybody knew the real reason couples went outside— and it didn't have anything to do with the air. Mercedes held her head high as she and Conner pushed their way through the crowd. The dancers parted to let them reach the doors leading out to the porch that ran the length of the Riding Academy.

Mercedes gasped as the chilly night air surrounded them.

"Will you be cold?" Conner asked. Mercedes took a

few steps to lead them out of sight of the ballroom doors. Then she turned around to face him.

"I don't know. Will I?" she asked.

Conner grinned and moved forward. He pulled her into his arms with a quick jerk.

"Not if I can help it," he said. And then he was kissing her again, long, deep kisses that left Mercy quivering from head to foot. She could feel his lips press against the place where her pulse beat in her throat. Felt him memorize the rhythm of her love for him. He pulled her head down onto his chest and held her close. Slowly, Mercy felt her heart beat return to normal.

"Mercy," Conner said finally. "There's something we have to talk about."

Instantly, Mercedes was alert.

"Mercy," Conner said again.

Gently, she pulled back from his embrace and stepped out of his arms. She turned her back to him and took a few more steps along the porch, trying to steady her ragged breathing—to deny the overwhelming sensation that something was about to go terribly wrong.

"What, Conner?" she whispered.

"It's about Elysian Fields," Conner answered.

Mercy could feel him watch her as she continued moving down the porch. Luminarias lined the side railing. The candle flames inside them twirled and flickered.

"What about them?" Mercedes asked.

"Jake Demos wasn't as understanding as I thought he'd be. He fired the band because I couldn't play tonight," Conner said. "Now we'll have to leave town right away to look for another gig."

Mercedes felt as if she were suffocating. With Conner, she had everything. Without him, she had nothing.

"Right away. You mean tonight?"

She heard Conner take a deep breath.

"I mean tonight," he said.

"No," Mercedes whispered. Conner crossed the distance between them and spun her around to face him.

"Why didn't you tell me?" she cried. "Why didn't you say something sooner?"

"I didn't want to spoil our last night together," Conner said. "I wanted you to have your beautiful evening before I told you."

"I won't let you go," she burst out passionately. She pounded her fists against his chest. "You can't leave me. I won't let you go," she said again.

"Mercy," Conner said soothingly. He reached out to brush away the tears that streamed unheeded down her face. "Mercy, honey, I'll find some way for us to be together. I promise I will."

"Just give me a little time, sweetheart," Conner pleaded. "That's all we need. Just a little time to work things out."

"Anything," she whispered. She held on tightly to the lapels of his coat. "Conner, I'll do anything to be with you. Anything. You know that. What do you want me to do? Tell me what to do to prove it."

Conner Egan went still as a statue. The light from the luminarias leaped up to stroke the planes of his face.

And then he was kissing her. Wildly and fiercely. Kissing Mercy as she'd never imagined being kissed, not even in her dreams.

"Mercy, Mercy," he murmured. His voice was thick with emotion. "You're mine, angel of Mercy. You can't ever leave me now. You're mine forever. Mine."

"Yes," she answered. "Yes."

"Tell me again," Conner begged her. "Let me know it's not a dream. Tell me again."

Mercedes gave a low trill of laughter.

"I love you, Conner Egan," she said. "I love you now and forever. I'll do anything to be with you. Just tell me what to do to prove it."

"Be with me," Conner said. He leaned down and kissed her. "Don't leave me tonight," he said against her mouth.

"I won't leave you, Conner," she said. "I won't ever leave you."

"I know you won't, my angel of Mercy."

Thirty-four

In her dreams, she could hear him. Laughing and laughing. She could feel his fingers closing ever tighter around her throat. He held her, face down, in the icy water.

"I told you what would happen if you tried to interfere," Conner Egan whispered. *"Why don't you give up while you're still alive? You'll never be strong enough to stand against me. Never."*

She struggled and fought, trying in vain to break his stranglehold. But the more she struggled, the stronger the grip around her neck became. In a moment, she knew it would be all over. She would die with the sound of Conner's laughter ringing in her ears as her lungs filled up with mud.

Andrea woke up gradually, swimming slowly to the surface of her nightmare the same way her face had floated to the top of the water just in time to save her life. She lay for a moment in the dark stillness of her room. She felt her body heavy against the mattress of the bed. She listened to her own breathing and the beating of her heart.

I'm alive, she thought. *I didn't die in the middle of the arena. I'm alive.*

She rolled her head slowly and painfully to one side. The red letter of her digital clock glowed in the darkness.

It was 6:00 A.M. Less than an hour before dawn.

She rolled her head back again and stared up at the ceiling. She was alive. But just barely. And if Conner Egan had his way, she'd be dead in an instant. Dead before she could make a stand against him. Dead before she could do anything that might save Mercy from a life of eternal damnation.

You could go back to sleep, part of her mind told her. Just pretend you never woke up. Pretend that stuff the doctor gave you was so powerful it kept you asleep until breakfast. Pretend you don't know anything.

And then I can have a new nightmare, she thought. *For the rest of my life, I can wake up every morning at 6:00 A.M. and pretend I don't feel anything, either.*

Gingerly, she sat up and eased her legs over the side of the bed. Her entire body felt like one big bruise. She tried not to listen as her muscles protested her quiet movements around the room. She shed her nightgown and pulled on her black jeans and a black turtleneck sweater. She laced hiking boots over thick wool socks and then opened the closet and took down the duffel bag she'd stowed away earlier.

Her fingers were stiff and clumsy. Her head pounded and her throat was dry. But the more she moved, the more certain she became. She had to get to the Night Owl Club and save Mercy.

Finally dressed, Andrea turned again to look at the digital clock. 6:15 A.M.

It would take her at least fifteen minutes to get from the Riding Academy to the Night Owl Club. There wasn't time to go to the kitchens for garlic. The farmer's almanac had

said the sun would rise at 6:57 A.M. Even if she could make it to the club by 6:30, that left her less than thirty minutes to figure out a way to rig a trap for Conner Egan.

Andy paused to shrug into her coat and strap on her watch. She set the watch alarm to go off at sunrise. Then she was easing open the door and moving silently down the corridor toward the back door of the Riding Academy on her way to the Night Owl Club.

Andrea could feel her body slow down as she approached the Cooper Hollow woods, reluctant to enter the place where Conner had so recently attacked her.

What if Jenny Demos were wrong? Andrea thought. What if Conner hadn't waited until dawn to turn Mercy into a vampire? He could be waiting for Andrea just inside the cover of the trees. Waiting to see whether or not she was brave enough—or stupid enough—to make a stand against him.

Andrea hesitated, just outside the tree line. For a moment, she couldn't go forward or back. Sweat poured down her face. The sound of her heartbeat was so loud a thousand Conners could have snuck up on her from a thousand different directions, and she never would have heard them.

She took a huge breath of cold, predawn air. She tried to picture Mercy in her mind. Not Mercy as she'd been these last two weeks. But the Mercy who'd been her friend for so many months. The Mercy whose friendship had helped ease Andrea's loneliness. The Mercy she loved. The Mercy she would save—at any cost.

Gripping her duffel bag tightly in one hand, Andrea plunged into the shadow of the Cooper Hollow woods. She

203

ran all the way to the Night Owl Club. The door was open when she got there.

Andrea burst through the front room and hurried to the dance floor. The interior of the Night Owl Club looked exactly as it had that morning. Nothing about it seemed to have changed. The candles still glowed in their glass holders; their enormous shadows still crept along the ceiling and walls.

Jenny Demos sat just where Andrea had left her. Andrea knew she'd been sitting there all night.

"Where is it," Andrea cried. She almost didn't recognize her own voice, it was so filled with passion. And with fear. "Where's Conner Egan's room?"

"You can't answer that question, Jenny," a harsh voice behind Andrea croaked.

Andrea whirled around. Behind her Jake Demos glowered in the doorway like an angry troll king guarding his treasure.

"You can't answer," Jake Demos said again. "You answer, and you'll interfere."

"It's a simple request for information," Jenny said calmly. "If I *don't* answer, I'll interfere." Andrea watched as Jake Demos' face turned an angry red.

Jenny rose and faced her father. "Those are the very words you used to justify telling Mercy where Conner's room was, Dad," Jenny said. "And I'll be *damned* if I'll let you get away with a double standard."

Her entire body shook with anger.

"If those words apply to you, they apply to me, too," Jenny continued passionately. "That means I can give Andy the information she needs."

"You may be damned," Jake Demos said quietly.

204

"I'll take that chance," Jenny replied. She turned to Andrea.

"Conner's room is upstairs, Andy. The room at the end of the hallway."

Jake Demos made a sudden movement, and then was still. Slowly, he walked to the nearest table and sank down into a chair.

"Where's the staircase?" Andrea asked. For a moment, neither Jenny nor her father answered.

"Where is it?" Andy shrieked. Jake Demos stirred.

"Behind the band platform," he said. Andrea stared at him, unable to believe he'd been the one to answer her question. Then she was running across the room.

"Young woman!" The harsh voice stopped her.

Andrea turned to face Jake Demos.

"You are entering a place filled with enormous power," the old man said. "Try to use your heart wisely."

"I will," she said, though she didn't understand the meaning of his words. "Thank you," she whispered.

Then she turned and put her foot on the bottom stair. She was halfway to the second story before she heard Jake Demos speak.

"Thank me—if you get back," he said.

Thirty-five

Andrea stood on the top of the second story landing and stared down the long hallway. She looked at her watch, pressing the tiny button on the side that made the face light up. It was 6:30 exactly. Gripping the duffel bag so tightly she thought every bone in her hand would break, she moved slowly toward the door at the end of the passage.

She had twenty-seven minutes to destroy Conner Egan.

The hallway was filled with strange sounds. Floorboards creaked. The scuffling sounds of rodents filled the shadows. Behind each door there seemed to be whispered conversations that suddenly stilled as she passed. Except for the room right next to Conner's; from behind that door came an anguished sobbing that never ceased.

The hall in front of her changed shape as Andrea moved. One moment the door to Conner's room was right next to her, the doorknob almost in her hand. The next, it was yards away. Although she could see no windows, a steady, foul-smelling breeze blew in her face.

I'll never get there, she thought. *I'll spend the rest of my life wandering in the hallway while Conner destroys Mercy to win his freedom.*

At the thought of Mercy, the hallway came into sudden focus. The sounds along the corridor stopped.

Use your heart, Andy thought, remembering Jake's advice. And she remembered his daughter's words: *Use your brain.*

She put out her hand and opened the door to Conner Egan's room.

The air in the room was thick and hot. The room felt alive, the walls pulsing like a human heart. The wounds in Andrea's neck began to ache and throb.

It took all the courage she had to shut the door behind her. Now she was alone in Conner Egan's room.

Except it wasn't Conner's room. It was Mercy's.

In horror, Andrea looked around her. The room was exactly like Mercy's at the Riding Academy in every detail. Desk, dresser, sink, and wash stand. Only the bed, in the far corner of the room, slipped in and out of focus. One moment it was Mercy's, spread with Granny Amberson's handmade quilt. The next, it was an old four-poster bed, spread with a quilt in faded shades of red, white, and blue.

As Andrea watched, the vision of Mercy's bed solidified and grew still. Now the room was ready for its new occupant.

Abruptly, the heat in the room increased, making the atmosphere stifling. Moisture oozed down the walls. She felt as if she were breathing through glue.

In the end, there really wasn't much choice. The room had only one window, at the end of Mercy's bed.

Andrea crossed the room swiftly and set down the duffel bag with a clunk. The window was covered by heavy drapes. Andrea seized them in the center and pulled them apart. Boards covered the inside of the window beneath the drapes. Around her, the room sighed and shuddered.

She unzipped the duffel bag, reaching for the crowbar. Still, the temperature in the room increased. Andrea's heartbeat pounded in her ears. The whispers she'd heard in the corridor had followed her to Conner's room. Now, they were all around her.

"Do it, Andrea," the whispering voices urged her. *"Don't hold back. Let your hatred of Conner Egan take control."*

The wounds in Andy's neck burned. She could hear Conner's taunts, his threats against her family. More than anything in the world, she longed to stride around the room, smashing everything in sight. She longed to destroy all evidence that he had ever existed. All evidence that he had tried to corrupt Mercy.

Andrea raised the crowbar above her head. She brought it down against the boards across the window. The boards remained in place and the whispers in the room increased in volume. One by one, they began to laugh at her.

Filled with rage, she raised the crowbar again. And then, from somewhere deep inside her, Andy heard her own voice. Her own brain telling her the truth.

If she destroyed things now, everything would be over. All it would take would be one glance for Conner to know that something was wrong. Chances are he'd leave immediately, taking Mercy with him.

Jake Demos was right, Andrea thought. There was more power here than she could possibly understand. And, if she wasn't careful, it would control her every move.

Slowly, she lowered the crowbar and put it back into the duffel bag. She removed the hammer and went for Mercy's desk chair. She dragged it across the room to the window and stood on it. Then she worked carefully at the nails holding the curtain rod in place. She jerked the nails outward, then slowly eased them back in. The curtain rods

were still up, but one hard yank on the curtains would pull them down.

She ran her hands along the boards nailed across the windows, wondering how long they'd been there. The only sign of age was a little bit of warping between them, as if the heat and moisture of the room had slowly shrunk the once solid wood. It wasn't much, but it was her only chance.

She had to do something that would bring those boards down. Something that would bring the light directly onto Conner and leave him no chance for escape.

Andrea attacked the nails holding the boards in place with the claw of her hammer. The nails shrieked as they tore through the old wood. Huge crimson drops welled up from the nail holes and ran along the length of the boards. As she worked, Andrea's hands were slowly stained with blood.

She jerked the top board forward until there was a small gap between it and the board below. Then she loosened the nails all down the window, working the boards as she went. When she was done, she climbed off the chair and took the longe tape out of her duffel bag.

Andrea checked her watch. It was 6:35 A.M. Her trip down the corridor had taken her a five full minutes. She knew her time was almost up. In order for Conner to re-enact his own demise, he and Mercy would have to arrive soon. He had to claim Mercy as his final victim just before dawn.

With trembling fingers, Andrea threaded the longe through the gaps she'd made between the boards. She looped it twice around the top board, stuffing the rope into the loop and knotting it tightly. She stepped back and

pulled down on the rope, testing its strength. The boards groaned as the leather between them bit and held.

And then she heard it. The sound of footsteps moving down the hall.

Desperately, she jerked the curtains back in place in front of the boards, hiding the trap she'd made. She returned Mercy's desk chair to its proper place with lightning speed. She grabbed the duffel bag and eased it open, taking from it her last two items of defense—the wooden cross and the stirrups still attached to their long length of leather.

Then she pushed the duffel bag into the only place there was to hide and crawled in after it. She tried not to think of how ridiculous she'd look if Conner Egan caught her. Andy was sure no vampire fighter had ever stooped this low, not even in the cheesiest movie.

She was hiding under the bed.

Silently, she eased herself down the length of the bed until she was at the very end, just beneath the window, thankful that this was Mercy's bed and not the old four-poster. The beds at the Riding Academy were built to hold a storage bin beneath them. Andy hoped that extra space would give her enough freedom to get out from under the bed in time to do whatever was necessary.

She didn't have to wait very long to find out.

Thirty-six

Conner Egan had cut it close.

The truth was that he hadn't wanted to bring Mercy to this room too soon. He knew he would have trouble holding back once he got her there so he had delayed, dancing the night away in the ballroom at the Riding Academy and then holding Mercy in his arms beneath the beautiful full moon.

But always, in the back of his mind, he'd been counting the moments until he could bring her here, until his years of waiting were complete. Conner's attention was focused so tightly on Mercy that the rest of the world ceased to exist for him.

Oh, my angel of Mercy, Conner thought as he led her down the hallway to his room at the Night Owl Club. *My revenge is going to taste so very, very sweet.*

He smiled down at her in the darkened corridor.

"We'll just go in for a moment," he said. "There are a few things I have to take care of."

Mercedes gasped as Conner opened the door.

"But, Conner, this is *my* room!" she said.

"Do you like it?" Conner asked. "I had it done as a special surprise for you."

Mercedes laughed as she stepped inside the room. She paused by the bed to run her hands across Granny Amberson's patchwork quilt.

"It's wonderful," she said. "But I don't understand why you'd go to so much trouble, why you'd have all of my belongings sent here. I thought you said we'd be leaving tonight."

"I said *I'd* be leaving, Mercy," Conner said. "You may be here for a while."

Mercedes' fingers faltered on the quilt. "I don't understand."

Conner danced across the room and caught her up in his arms. He twirled Mercedes round and round until she was breathless with laughter and excitement.

"Tell me," Conner commanded as he spun her around. "Tell me how much you love me."

"I love you forever," she gasped. Gradually, Conner's movements slowed. He stood with Mercedes near the head of the bed, his arms wound tightly around her.

"And what will you do for me, Mercy," Conner asked. "What will you do to prove you love me?"

"Anything," Mercedes whispered. "Anything."

Conner smiled. "Yes, my angel of Mercy," he said softly. "Yes, you will."

Slowly, passionately, he kissed her. He could feel her body grow heavy in his arms. He trailed his kisses across her face and down her neck. He lingered at the spot where her pulse beat, tasting the pulse of his freedom.

Then he stretched his mouth wide and buried his teeth in her throat.

She was strangling. Helpless in the grip of some powerful animal. She could feel its teeth in her neck tearing

212

through her skin. The pain was so intense she was afraid she would faint. But if she fell, she knew that whatever held her would rip her throat out.

Desperately, Mercedes beat against the thing that held her, trying to break its grip. Conner, she thought. Had the thing already taken Conner?

Frenzied now, determined to save her love at any cost, she struck out, raking her fingers down her attacker's face. Against all odds, she managed to get out a single word.

"Conner," she said.

Abruptly the thing released her. Mercedes staggered back and her legs gave way. Slowly, she slid to the ground at the foot of the bed. She stared in disbelief at the figure towering over her.

Blood dripped from its open jaws and stained the front of its snow white shirt. It had hair the color of a snow storm and eyes that glowed like green jewels in its bloody face. Incredibly, it began to laugh.

"What's the matter, my little angel of Mercy?" the monster said. "Don't you recognize me?"

The thing in front of her was Conner Egan.

Mercedes' head began to swim. Her neck felt like it was on fire. She reached up to press her hand against the pain. Her hand came away bloody. She lifted her hand, palm up, toward the thing that stood before her.

"That's right, Mercy," Conner said. "That's your blood. And soon it will be mine. All of it. Then you will be the vampire, and I'll be free."

Mercedes managed one last word.

"Vampire," she said.

* * *

213

Andrea had heard enough. She'd meant to wait until her watch alarm went off, telling her it was sunrise. But she couldn't bear to hear Mercy in pain. To hear Conner tormenting her.

Andrea no longer cared what time it was. She no longer cared if she was using her brain or her heart. All she cared about was getting out from under that bed to protect her friend.

She angled herself against the wall, trying to get some extra leverage. Then she pushed off, shooting her head and shoulders out from under the bed. She scrambled desperately with her legs, trying to get all the way out while she still had the element of surprise. The minute her legs were free, she scrambled to her feet.

In one hand, she held up the wooden cross. In the other, she clutched the length of stirrup leather.

"Mercy," she screamed. She surged forward, trying to grab Mercedes by the shoulder, but the stirrup leather got in her way. Andrea couldn't move Mercy back under the window without Mercy's help. And Mercy wasn't going anywhere.

"Mercy," Andrea cried. "Listen to me. You've got to get behind me! Get behind me!"

Mercedes still refused to move. Conner Egan began to laugh.

"My poor Andrea," he said. "You don't really believe you can stop me with that stupid wooden cross do you?" He took a step forward.

Andrea moved closer to Mercedes and raised the cross. In spite of his words, Conner hissed and fell back. Andrea released her grip on the stirrup, letting it fall to the floor. She twisted her wrist, winding the end of the leather across her palm.

214

For a moment, Andrea and Conner faced each other across the room.

"It won't work, Andrea Burgess," Conner taunted softly. "You'll never make it out of this room alive."

"You're the one who's not going to make it, Conner," Andrea said. "Mercy and I are walking out of here together. As real human beings.

"But first, I'm going to send you straight to hell."

Without warning, she surged forward, placing the wooden cross in Mercy's arms. Then she scrambled frantically backward, her free hand reaching for the heavy drapes. With one swift yank, she brought them tumbling down. The leather between the boards and the rope that would bring them down were plainly visible.

With a snarl of rage, Conner started toward her. He made a wide circuit around Mercedes and the cross resting in her arms. Mercedes' eyes followed Conner as he moved toward Andrea, but her body remained motionless.

Andrea pivoted back toward Conner and let the length of stirrup leather fly. It sailed across the room on its way to completing a perfect circle. The heavy metal stirrup caught Conner full in the face.

Screaming with rage, Conner reached out and pulled hard on the leather line. Andrea was caught, the end of the stirrup leather still wound tightly around her wrist. She fell face down on the floor, the wind knocked out of her. With an ugly laugh, Conner began to drag her across the room like he was reeling in a fish.

He didn't stop until Andrea was lying helpless at his feet.

From where she sat against the bed, she could see them. Conner leaning over Andrea. His face filled with anger

and delight. Andrea lay prone on the floor in front of him and didn't move at all.

"I have you now, Andrea Burgess," Mercedes could hear him say. "Do you remember what I promised you would happen if you tried to interfere with me?"

He flipped Andrea over onto her back. Her face was bloody from where she'd hit the floor. Her eyes blinked rapidly, as if she were trying to focus.

What does she want to see? Mercy wondered. *All there is to look at here is death.*

"I promised you would die, Andrea," Conner continued, echoing Mercedes' thoughts. "And I promised your family would die. I'm sorry you won't be around to know that I've killed them. But don't worry. You can take my word for it. They'll be dead. Every last one of them. And they'll all know it was because of you."

No, Mercedes thought in sudden horror. *No.*

She looked at Conner's pale blond hair, the end of the scarlet ribbon trailing down one side of his neck. She saw again the back of that head as it had turned toward her. Just moments before she'd found the dead girl in the graveyard.

The dead girl, Mercedes thought. Everywhere he goes, he brings death. Soon Andrea would be dead and her family would be dead. Because Mercedes had refused to listen. Everything Andrea had said about Conner was true.

"Mercy," Andrea croaked. "Mercy, listen to me."

Conner laughed. "Yes, listen to her, Mercy," he mocked. His gaze flickered over Mercedes propped up against the bed.

"These words will be the last ones your friend Andrea will ever speak. And almost the last ones you'll ever hear. As a human being that is."

"Listen for my alarm, Mercy," Andrea whispered. "Pull the rope. Listen for my alarm and pull the rope by the window."

"So that was the plan," Conner said. "Death by sunlight. How pathetic. Who suggested that method of attack, Jenny Demos? But of course, she couldn't come with you to help out, could she?

"You picked the wrong friends, Andrea. And now it's time to pay for your mistake."

Conner looked across the room at Mercedes. "Say goodbye to your very best friend, Mercy," he said. "You're never going to see her alive again."

He crouched over Andrea like a vulture picking over a corpse. With a great cry of triumph, he leaned down and seized her by the throat.

Andrea began to scream, a high thin wail that Mercedes knew she would never forget. Andrea's body arched in a series of painful spasms, and then lay still. Soon, the only sound was Conner Egan's swallows as he sucked out Andrea's life blood.

Andrea, Mercedes thought. Andrea, her only friend, who was proving her friendship by paying with her life.

And then she heard it. The small, insistent beep of Andrea's watch alarm.

It was 6:57 A.M. The sun was rising over Cooper Hollow, New York.

Slowly, painfully, Mercedes looked away from Conner and Andrea and focused on what was behind her. She saw the window covered by old boards. And, running like a snake between them, the leather longe tied fast to the rope.

What had Andrea told her?

Listen for the alarm and pull the rope.

Mercedes' body felt like lead. She couldn't get her legs

217

to move. She flopped over onto her side. As she began to pull herself along the floor toward the window. The wooden cross hit the floor.

Conner Egan lifted his head. His muzzle dripped with Andrea's blood. Beside him on the floor, Andrea drew a long, rattling breath.

She's still alive, Mercedes thought. *I've got to make sure she stays that way.* The wounds on her neck sent blood pulsing down her arms. She crawled along a floor slippery with her own blood.

Until she reached the rope.

With bloody arms she reached up and caught hold of the bottom of the rope. Using all her strength, Mercedes pulled. The nails holding the boards in place moaned and shrieked. The walls of the room shuddered and wailed, but the boards held fast.

Conner Egan began to laugh.

"You'll never do it, Mercy," he mocked. He rose to his feet and started toward her. "Your friend Andy was the strong one. And look what I've done to *her.*"

Mercedes heard Andrea take another breath.

"You're weak, Mercy," Conner said. "Stupid and weak. Just what I was looking for. And now you're mine. Nothing you can do is going to stop me. Nothing."

"I hate you," Mercedes whispered. She wound the rope around her arms, using it to haul herself painfully to her feet. She swayed as she faced Conner, but she wound the rope even tighter.

"I hate you," she whispered hoarsely.

And then Mercedes was rushing forward, running toward Conner at full speed. She held her arms straight out in front of her, as if she would embrace him. And she took the rope along with her.

218

The longe Andrea had threaded through the boards across the window took the full force of Mercedes' run. Behind her, the rope pulled taut. The leather bit deep into the boards. The old wood creaked and groaned. Then, with a final shriek, the nails in the top board began to give way. A tiny band of sunlight appeared through the window.

"No," Conner Egan cried. He stood transfixed, unable to take his eyes away from the light.

Mercedes fell to her knees as the rope jerked her backward. She leaned forward and began to crawl across the floor. The rope scraped against Conner's teeth marks in her neck. Still she moved forward.

"You are evil," Mercedes whispered. "You are evil, and I will destroy you."

"Mercy, no," Conner cried. "Mercy, please, sweetheart. I love you. Don't do this to me. I love you!"

Mercedes put her hands on the rope where it ran across her shoulder and pulled with all her strength—all the strength of her love for Andrea, all her desire to defeat the evil that threatened to destroy her friend.

One by one, the boards across the window splintered, leaving Conner Egan standing in the bright morning sun.

He opened his mouth to scream, but not a sound came out.

"Happy Valentine's Day, Conner," Mercedes said.

Conner's body began to swell, as if the blood of all his victims was rising out of him. Blood oozed from under his fingernails and dripped from the ends of his hair. It filled his eyes and ran down his face in a steady stream of crimson tears. He began to convulse, and the room around them began to shake.

And then, the body that had once been Conner Egan blew apart, showering the room with blood. Where his

body struck the walls, they began to crumble and fall away. Sobbing, Mercedes untangled herself from the rope and crawled across the room toward Andrea.

"We did it, Andy," she cried. She cradled her friend's head in her lap as the room disintegrated around them. "We did it," she said again. "We killed him."

Andrea opened her eyes and smiled at her.

"I knew you would do it, Mercy," she said.

Then she closed her eyes. Mercedes bent over her, glad they were together at the end of the world.

Thirty-seven

Mercedes and Andrea walked through the old grave-yard. They moved slowly among the headstones. It was taking Andrea a long time to recover her strength.

The two friends were heroes in the Cooper Hollow community. Belatedly, the police had come to believe that Conner Egan had killed the girl Mercedes had found in the old graveyard, and that Mercedes had been his next intended victim. They were amazed that Andrea had been brave enough to try to save her friend. They were even more amazed that the two girls' escape had been successful.

Andrea and Mercedes never knew what the Demoses had told Detective Priestly, but his questions for them had been brief. The other members of Elysian Fields had vanished from Cooper Hollow as if they'd never existed. Slowly, things began to return to normal.

Throughout the weeks of their recovery, Mercedes had struggled to find a way to talk to Andrea. How did you thank someone for being the sort of friend who would give her life for you? How did you say you were sorry for making such a sacrifice necessary?

Over and over again, Mercedes had wondered how she

could have mistaken for true love what Conner offered her. She still hadn't been able to come up with an answer.

Now, the friends came to a stop at the place where Mercy had discovered Elaine Taylor. Together, they stared at the headstone sticking out of the snow. The inscription on it read:

Richard Campbell. 1770-1793. Rest in Eternal Peace.

Slowly, Mercedes reached into her pocket, and brought out the heart-shaped locket. It was the only thing left of Conner Egan.

"What will you do with it?" Andrea finally asked.

"I think I'll bury it," Mercedes answered. "That seems right, somehow, don't you think? I'll come back here when the ground is soft enough." She looked over at Andrea and smiled. "It'll be the last time I sneak around after hours, I promise."

Andrea smiled back. She reached over and took the locket out of Mercedes' hand. She opened the clasp of the golden heart. Nestled inside were several strands of pale blond hair.

"Do you suppose he gave it to her?" Andrea asked. "Whoever turned him into a vampire?"

"We'll never know," Mercedes answered. She took the locket back from Andrea and turned it slowly in her hands. "It's hard to feel sorry for him, but I guess he couldn't help himself. He didn't have anyone to save him." She closed the locket and returned it to her pocket. "He wasn't as lucky as I was. I had you."

Andrea smiled again, but her eyes were filled with tears.

"Hey, guess what?" she said, before Mercedes could say any more. She linked her arm through Mercy's as they started back toward the Riding Academy. "My mom wants

222

you to come home with me for spring break. Will your parents let you?"

"*Let* me!" Mercy laughed. "They'll be packing my bags and filling out a change of address card before you know it."

"It'll be so cool," Andrea said. "I'll be able to show you all the places in the pictures." She paused and glanced at Mercedes. "Bill will be home," she said.

Mercedes laughed. "Just so long as he doesn't put any snakes in my bed," she answered. "Oh, Andy, look," she cried suddenly. She knelt by the side of the path, her face filled with delight.

There, pushing bravely through the snow, were cluster after cluster of tiny white flowers. Granny Amberson had taught Mercedes to recognize them.

Mercedes lifted her joyous face to Andrea.

"Snowdrops," she said.

The first flowers of spring.

●

NOW OPEN!
THE NIGHT OWL CLUB

Pool Tables, Video Games, Great Munchies,
Dance Floor, Juke Box, *Live* Bands On Weekend.

* * *

Bring A Date Or Come Alone . . .

* * *

Students From Cooper High School,
Hudson Military Academy,
Cooper Riding Academy for Girls
Especially Welcome . . .

* * *

Located Just Outside Of Town.
Take Thirteen Bends Road,
Or Follow Path Through Woods.

* * *

Don't Let The Dark Scare You Away . . .

* * *

Jake and Jenny Demos-proprietors
Teen club, no alcohol served.

sense of uneasiness seemed to pervade the place. Even the location made no sense—in the middle of the woods and not on a direct road leading into town.

But Julia thought it was the perfect place for them to remain safe and undetected. Though gentlemen fought for their honor often enough, the practice of dueling was still frowned upon in the new United States. Winning your duel, as Conner had, was no guarantee of future safety. The Owl's Head was isolated, separated from the country town of Cooper Hollow by dense woods and dangerous, winding roads. Whatever happened at the Owl's Head or in its vicinity would remain a secret.

As Conner and Julia came into view, a figure detached itself from the tavern and moved silently toward them across the snow. Conner was surprised to see that it was the innkeeper himself who had come to take their horses. Without a word, the man helped Julia dismount and waited patiently for Conner to fling his leg across the saddle and slide effortlessly to the ground. Conner saw the innkeeper's eyes flicker briefly over Richard Campbell's riderless horse, but the man made no remark. Conner paused to remove his saddlebag and toss it over his shoulder. Then, taking Julia's arm, he strode purposefully toward the Owl's Head Inn.

The stars above their heads had just begun to pale. It was almost dawn.

Inside Julia hurried on ahead of him, taking the stairs two at a time. Conner could feel his heart begin to pound inside his chest. Torn between his desire for Julia and his desire to escape the Owl's Head and all that had happened there, he hurried after her. By the time he reached Julia's second story room, she was ready and waiting for him.

She was standing in the middle of the room, her face

glowing, her arms open wide and beckoning. She was dressed like a bride in flowing, luxurious white. On her breast was the golden heart-shaped locket he had given her in token of their love. All Conner's thoughts of leaving the Owl's Head vanished.

"Oh, my Conner," Julia cried as he started toward her. She caught him in a fierce embrace. "My Conner you have done what no one else has dared. You have set me free!" Conner tightened his arms around her, holding Julia so close he could hardly breathe. The grip of his emotions was so powerful he was incapable of speech.

"Unless . . ." Julia lifted her head to stare up into Conner's face. He watched as her huge, dark eyes began to fill with fear. "You meant it, didn't you Conner? What you said at the lake?" Her breath caught in her throat and, suddenly, she tore herself away from him.

"Oh, my God," she cried, burying her face in her hands. "What have I done? I've trusted my life to you and now you'll leave me. You'll abandon me in this terrible place. All your words of love were lies. Only lies!"

"Julia, for heaven's sake!" Conner crossed the distance between them in two long strides and pulled her back into his arms. He could feel her tremble at his touch. He stroked her beautiful dark hair and then tilted back her head.

"Listen to me, Julia," Conner Egan said. "I love you. I love you now and forever. I'll do anything in the world for you." Julia sobbed and buried her face against his neck.

"Julia, my beautiful Julia," Conner murmured, stroking her hair. "You'll feel better when we're far away from this terrible place. We're free now, Julia. Free to live our lives together. Free!"

As if to give a final fanfare to Conner's words, the inn's

rooster began to crow in the yard outside. In a moment, it would be dawn.

Julia gave a sigh and relaxed in Conner's arms. She seemed to melt into him. He could feel her breath as she pressed her lips against his neck. Conner began to feel that time was standing still. He would stand here forever, holding the woman he loved in his arms. Now he could feel her teeth as she ran them back and forth across his neck. She nipped him with playful little bites and Conner could feel his pulse accelerate. Then slowly, tantalizingly, Julia nuzzled her face against his neck and sank her teeth deep into his throat.

Pain shot through Conner. A pain unlike anything he'd ever experienced. The world began to spin and lurch. He struggled against Julia, trying to force her away from his neck. But she only increased her grip, burrowing her face further into his throat. The loving woman he'd held in his arms a moment before had become a monster. Some ferocious demon made entirely of lips and teeth, determined to cling to him at any cost. He heard a horrible sound, as if some disgusting animal were guzzling and slurping at a food trough. And realized it was the sound of Julia gulping down his blood.

With a great cry, Conner grasped Julia by the hair and forced her head back. Back and back he forced it, until he thought her neck would surely snap. Julia's eyes glittered with a horrible light. Her lips and teeth, the ones Conner had always thought so beautiful, were covered entirely with blood.

His blood. Her face was smeared with it. It ran down her chin and stained the front of her beautiful white dress. Snarling like a wild animal, Julia broke free and staggered back across the room. Conner stood for a moment, sway-

11

ing like an old tree in the wind. He could feel the blood pulse from his neck, running down his arm and across his chest. Then, slowly, his legs gave way and he sank to his knees. Across the room, the woman who called herself Julia McKenzie began to laugh.

"Free!" she mocked. She licked her lips and ran her tongue across her teeth. "Oh, yes, Conner Egan, one of us is free. But I'm afraid it isn't you, my love." She moved a little closer to him, swaying from side to side as she laughed.

"My dear, sweet love," she said, her voice a horrible parody of what it had been. "My Conner, who will do anything for me and love me forever. Shall I tell you just what you and your love have done?

"You have freed me from this." Julia gestured around the room. And, for the first time, Conner noticed the strangeness of it. The boards across the window. The drapes, thick enough to cut out any chance of light. The air of the room was heavy and hot. The walls began to pulse and shudder. As Conner watched, every item in the room that belonged to Julia slowly began to fade away. Slowly, inexorably, Conner watched as, piece by piece, the room became his. His desk, his wardrobe and dressing table. His four-poster bed, with the red, white, and blue quilt that had been his grandmother's. In every detail, it was his room. The room where he had hoped to bring Julia as a bride.

The room was now unbearably hot. A heat which drained away the last of Conner's strength. He hardly resisted as Julia crossed to him. Slowly, gently, she settled herself on the floor and drew his head into her lap.

"I'm sorry for you, my brave Conner," she said, stroking the hair from his eyes. Conner looked up at her, this woman for whom he had killed a man. Her face was shiny with

12